CHAS WILLIAMSON
Paradise Series: Book Five

CHRISTMAS
in Paradise

Print ISBN: 978-1-64649-132-2

eBook ISBN: 978-1-64649-133-9

 Year of the Book
135 Glen Avenue
Glen Rock, PA 17327

Dedication

Christmas in Paradise is dedicated to the woman who shares not just my name, but my past, my present and my future. The memories we share are a testament to the life we've built. And what we've made together is the stuff of dreams, of fairy tales. And because of you, we're living happily ever after.

God has blessed me more than anyone else I've ever known, and the greatest blessing I've received is your love. The fact that He brought us together so early in life just magnifies our blessings.

Hand in hand and side by side, we've conquered the world together. And when this life is over, I know we'll be together for all eternity, because honestly, I'd probably get in trouble without you there to guide me. And there's no one else I'd rather have by my side for eternity.

Any heroine my mind could ever create could never compare to you, for to me, *you are perfect*.

I loved you the moment I first saw you, and in a million years, the only thing that will change is that I will love you even more.

And as you taught me, *true love lasts forever*.

Acknowledgments

To God, for the love You placed in my heart and soul.

To my best friend and soulmate, for always believing in me. With your help, I've fulfilled my two greatest dreams—love and writing.

To my father, for teaching me how to tell tall tales and interesting stories.

To my beta readers, Janet, Sarah, Connie, Mary and Bekah for your help in making *Christmas in Paradise* the best it could be.

To Demi, for all your assistance, guidance, support and friendship. You've helped me become a published writer.

To my fans and friends, for always believing in me. I receive no greater compliment than when you read my stories.

The Families of Paradise

The Lapp Clan

Aubrey Lapp – Connor's wife
Connor Lapp – Aubrey's husband
Eli Jamison – Rachel's ex-fiancé
Greiston (Grey) Lapp – Aubrey and Connor's adopted
    daughter
Isaac "Devo" Golden – Aubrey's step-brother
Leslie Lapp – Connor's sister
Mary "Mimes" Lapp – Leslie and Connor's mother
Rachel Domitar – Leslie and Aubrey's close friend
Rebecca Stoltzfus – Leslie's Amish neighbor

The Rohrer Clan

Daisy Elliot – Joe's close friend and co-worker
Frannie Rohrer, Joe's sister
Jake Elliot – Daisy's husband
Joseph Rohrer, MD

The Campbell Clan

Ashley Campbell – Harry's wife
Edmund Campbell – Henry's brother
Ellie Campbell – Henry's wife
Harry Campbell – Henry's brother, Ashley's husband
Henry Campbell – co-owner of Campbell Farms, Ellie's
    husband
Sophie Miller – owner of the Tea Room, Henry & Ellie's
    best friend

The Espenshade Clan

Didi Phillips-Zinn – Hannah's closest friend

Hannah Espenshade – Sam's wife

Jenna Espenshade – Sam's sister, Kim's ex-fiancée (deceased)

Jenna Lynne Espenshade - Sam and Hannah's youngest daughter

Kim Landis – Jenna's ex-fiancé

Mickey Campeau – Riley's husband

Riley Campeau – Sam's older sister

Sam Espenshade – Hannah's husband

Get exclusive
never-before-published content!

www.chaswilliamson.com

A Paradise Short Story

Download your free copy of
Skating in Paradise today!

Prelude

Nine Years Ago

Rachel Domitar checked out the reflection in the mirror, the face of her best friend Leslie Lapp shadowing over her shoulder. "How do I look?"

Leslie's eyes were happy, that perpetual smile gracing her face. "I can honestly say, I've never seen a more beautiful bride." Leslie squeezed Rachel's hand. "I'm so ecstatic for you."

Rachel nodded. "I do look kind of pretty, don't I?"

Leslie giggled. "Yep, you clean up well. Where's he taking you for the honeymoon?"

Eli's face flashed before Rachel's eyes. "Barbados."

"Barbados? Wow, sounds like heaven. Then you get to come back to... New Jersey." Leslie giggled. "Sorry to hear that." Rachel knew her friend was going to tease her. "Won't that be a letdown?"

The bride-to-be shook her head. "Never. Heaven is anywhere that we're together." She turned and took the hands of her dear friend. "Thanks for sharing today with me, for being my maid of honor."

"My pleasure, though I kinda wish you were marrying my brother, Connor."

Rachel humphed. "Don't you call him Connie? Come on, lady. I'd never marry a man with a girl's name. I wanted a man's man. Besides, do you think there's something wrong with Eli?"

"No, no. He's pretty perfect in my book. I was just thinking it would be nice to have you as my sister, that's all."

"You already have a sister."

Leslie's smile dimmed. "Lisa's not really the sister type."

Rachel remembered their talks about Leslie's sibling. Both Leslie and her brother Connor referred to their elder sister, Lisa, as the wild child of the family. "She can't be that bad."

Swallowing hard, Leslie replied, "I don't want to talk about her today. Let's reminisce about the two of you. Tell me the story of how you two met."

"You already know it because you saw it first-hand."

"Aww, come on Rach. Tell me again, please?"

Once more, the vision of the tall, well-built man she loved came to her. "It was our first year at Alvernia. He worked at the convenience store close to the campus. The first time I saw him, it was like... wow. I couldn't take my eyes off of him. I used to find reasons to frequent there, just to see him."

"Yeah, yeah. I remember that. Fast forward to the cool part."

Rachel fanned her face. *Because of the heat or the thought of Eli?* "I stopped by the store late one wintery Sunday night. Eli should have been working, but he wasn't behind the counter. Disappointed, I started to walk back to the dorm alone. Before I'd gone one block, I noticed this weird guy following me. He began talking, trying to get my attention. Kept making flirtatious comments. I cut down an alley, trying to lose him. Much to my horror, I discovered it was a dead end."

Leslie's eyes were wide, but her face reflected the anticipation because she knew how the story ended. "Then what?"

"I reached into my pocket, grabbing my room key. It was the only thing I had to defend myself with. When I turned around, he was right there before me and the jerk had a nasty smirk on his face."

Leslie nodded. "Go on."

"As the guy moved closer, a quick movement behind him caught my attention. It was Eli. He ran in between the weirdo and me, turning to face my assailant. Eli took my hand and told him, 'Get away from my girl.' He followed up with, 'Honey, I've been looking for you. Let's go home.' The jerk split. Eli turned to me and said he'd been in the back. A co-worker told Eli he'd missed me. Eli revealed he was looking forward to seeing me that night, so he came to search for me. Not only did he walk me to my room, he asked me out."

Leslie laughed. "And the rest is history. You're lucky, girl."

Warmth flooded Rachel's chest. "I am. He's the only man I've ever been with or wanted to date. I love him to the moon and back, you know?"

Before Leslie could answer, there was a soft knock on the door. Leslie opened it. "Eli? You can't be here. Don't you know it's bad luck to see your bride before you two get married?"

Rachel retreated to a corner of the room, out of sight of the open door.

Eli's voice was soft. "I know all that, but I need to talk to Rachel. Now."

Leslie turned to Rachel, eyes questioning. Eli's words flowed to her from around the door. "It's real important, Rach. Please?"

Rachel nodded and Leslie backed away from the opening. The door swung wide and Eli entered. It struck her as odd that he was wearing jeans this close to the service. While his eyes were locked on Rachel's, his voice was directed at her friend. "Give us a few minutes, okay?"

"Sure. I'll be in the hallway." Leslie left the room.

Icy tendrils crawled across Rachel's shoulders. A direct contrast to the hands holding her cheeks— Eli's. "You look so beautiful." His eyes were suddenly watery. "I still remember the first time I saw you. It was a Sunday night. You bought a pint of Rocky Road and a Diet Coke. And I fell in love with you right then and there."

"What's going on?"

"When you walked out, it was so hard to watch you go. I willed you to come back. Wanted to know everything about you." Eli's hands dropped down until they were holding hers.

"You're scaring me."

"And then, when you walked back in a couple of days later, I knew you were the woman I wanted to spend my life with."

Rachel could sense the dread rolling off of him. "Eli..."

The suddenness of his lips against hers was surprising as he drew her tightly into his arms. Wet and warm, his mouth caressed hers. He hugged her tightly and whispered into her ear, "Run away with me, right this second."

Pushing away, Rachel's hands framed his face. "We're getting married in less than an hour."

Eli winced. "We can't."

A bucket of ice water couldn't have chilled her more. "What?"

A knock sounded on the door. "Mr. Jamison? We need to leave right away."

Rachel felt her lips tremble as she searched his face. "Who's that out there? Are you in trouble?"

Eli nodded. "Remember when I went to New York City with my friends a couple of months ago?"

Rachel noted her hands were shaking, but was unsure if the trembling originated from her or Eli. "Y-yes?"

"I witnessed something while I was there."

"What?"

He slowly shook his head. "I can't tell you, baby. I explained to the police what I saw and they told me I couldn't tell anyone. And because of what I saw that night, I have to go away. There are people who want to hurt me. And I'm worried if I stay, they might come after you."

I don't understand. "So you're leaving?"

Eli's jaw was quivering. "I have to, unless..."

"Unless what?"

His grip on her hands intensified. "Come away with me. It'll be the two of us, forever, just like we dreamed about." A sadness filled his eyes. "But you'll have to leave everything behind. Never see your family or friends again."

A pounding sound interrupted them. "Ten seconds, Jamison."

Rachel wiped her cheeks. "Leave everyone behind? Just like that?"

He kissed her hands. "Just the two of us... forever and always."

It was so hard to breathe. "But, but..."

The door flew open. Two men in suits entered the room. A tall, dark man was obviously in charge. "We need to move, immediately. Let's go, Jamison."

Eli squeezed her hands again. "Come with me, Rach. Please?"

So sudden, so confusing. "Can I have time to think it over?"

Eli's eyes darkened. "I shouldn't have come." Droplets of moisture appeared on his cheeks. His trembling hands touched her chin and his lips softly brushed against her cheek. "Remember us, and how much we loved each other. Goodbye."

Before Rachel could move, the three men disappeared. Leslie was suddenly in the room, her arms wrapped around Rachel. Leslie's embrace held her up because her knees would no longer support her. The room started to spin and everything grew confusing. A throbbing ache began in her chest. The pain was almost unbearable, right in the spot where her broken heart now lived. The room grew dark and she saw no more.

Chapter One

April

The vehicle shuddered again, this time almost throwing Leslie Lapp against the steering wheel. "Come on, George. I know you're tired, but just get me home. You owe me that much, after all the gas I've put in you—only high test, mind you. Not a drop of regular—ever." Her beloved Suburban, the one she'd named after country singer George Jones, was on its last legs. *Should have traded you in when my brother Connor suggested it.* But George had been faithful for the last 300,000 miles, so Leslie held onto him.

The vehicle jolted hard a final time and began to slow. Leslie stepped on the gas pedal. While the engine roared, the sport utility continued to decelerate. There was no choice but to steer the three-ton behemoth onto the side of the road.

He stopped loving me today... "Thanks, buddy. So much for being a faithful companion." Safely off the road, she punched in her brother's phone number. He answered on the second ring.

"Hey, sis. What's shaking?"

"George is, well he used to be. I believe my faithful companion finally gave up the ghost. Is there any way you can come pick me up?"

"First, are you safe?"

"Relatively, if you call sitting along the Lincoln Highway outside of Coatesville safe. Would you be able to come get your beloved older sister in her moment of need?"

Connor hesitated. "Aubrey and I are on our way to the obstetrician. We can come after our appointment, but it might be a good hour and a half before we get there. Hold up a second." Leslie could hear her sister-in-law's voice on the other end. Her brother spoke up again. "Aubrey said we'll cancel, but it will still be close to an hour until we arrive. That okay?"

They'd skip the checkup for me? "No. You need to make sure the baby's fine. I'll call triple-A. Maybe they can give me a lift."

"Are you sure? Wish there was something I could do. I feel bad."

"And you should, Connie." That was the term of endearment she'd given him years ago. "After all I've done for you, since birth, I might remind you. Gave you a job, room and board, helped you with Aubrey..." Her lips curled. Leslie and Connor teased each other relentlessly.

A loud yawn filled her ear, obviously a forced one. "Oh my, look at the time. Just wondering, are you done with the guilt trip, Leslie? Seriously, anything I can do to help?"

"There is. Take care of your family. However, if not being there for me in my time of need bothers your conscience, if you have one, feel free to name the baby after me. But only if it's a girl."

After hanging up, Leslie called for a tow truck. Old George rocked particularly hard when a speeding tractor trailer whizzed by close enough she could count the individual rivets on the trailer. *Might be safer outside, I guess.* She climbed out and found a comfortable grass clump to sit on. The early spring's musty odor of decaying organic matter filled the air. While a mild April breeze danced among the still bare branches above her head, the threatening skies looked like they might open up any second.

The cell phone in her pocket vibrated. *Rachel.* "Hey, Rach. How's it going?"

"This a bad time?"

"Nope. Just doing yoga along the highway."

"Huh? Leslie, you're really weird. Do you know that?"

She couldn't help but laugh. "Sorry. The Suburban decided to stage a sit-down protest, so I'm twiddling my thumbs, waiting for a tow truck."

"Oh, okay. Whatever. Hey, I really need a friend. Can we talk?"

Rachel and Leslie had been close since their freshman year at Alvernia College. Only her brother Connor and his wife, Aubrey, were closer to her than Rachel. "Absolutely. What's going on?"

The sound of sniffling preceded the voice. "We had a staff meeting yesterday morning and I was *instructed* to report to the school board meeting last night."

"Instructed to report? What do you mean?"

"The board announced their decision. They've decided to drop all non-essential courses from the curriculum—music, chorus, shop, home ec and drama."

"What? Why would they do that?"

"They're trying to cut costs. Oh, the board cited plenty of reasons—increased wages, dwindling tax base, low SAT scores, teachers' pension costs, returning to the basics—you name it."

"How does this affect you? They'll move you into a different position, won't they?"

"Nope. I'm gone. Unemployed after the school year ends."

The cars driving east on the other side of the highway all had their lights on. *Rain's coming.* "I'm sorry. What are you going to do? Look for another teaching position?"

A small sob reached her ear. "I need a change. Pretty sure my teaching career has run its course. And there's absolutely no reason to stay here in Jersey anymore. Everyone I ever loved either moved away or died."

Leslie's heart went out to her friend. First the loss of Eli, then her mother's death and finally her dad had passed, just two months ago.

"Hey, Rach. Why don't you come down and hang with me for a while? We'll figure this out together."

"I don't want to be an imposition."

"Stop it." Her mind drifted back to a particularly miserable weekend years ago. "Do you remember the pledge we made to each other during our freshman year, after that stupid party?"

More sniffling. "Maybe…"

The skies opened and the deluge soaked her to the skin within seconds. "We promised to always, always, always be there for each other, no matter what the world threw at us."

Leslie ran until she stood behind George. She desperately wanted to climb inside where it would be dry, but the string of traffic was seemingly endless. And to make matters worse, each passing vehicle sent a wave of road spray to coat her.

"Are you okay? Sounds like you're standing in the shower."

"Hold on. It's pouring and I can't get in the driver's side."

"Then climb in the passenger seat, silly."

Leslie smacked her head. "Duh! Why didn't I think of that?"

Rachel laughed through her tears. "Because you've always been easily distracted by bright colors and squirrels."

Leslie opened the door, swept her belongings off the seat and climbed in. "Okay, I'm a little drier. Where were we?"

"You were lifting me out of the gutter where I'm wallowing in self-pity."

It was Leslie's turn to laugh. "I don't know about changing careers. You always were pretty good at being a drama queen."

"Har-de har har. Were you serious about being up for a visit?"

"Of course." Blurry red lights diffracted through the windshield. A vehicle had pulled off the road in front of her. Leslie's mouth went dry when she realized the car was backing toward her. She could see the reverse lights grow large as it approached the Suburban. "Rach, a car just pulled over ahead of me. It's backing up. Right in front of me!"

"Your tow truck?"

"Uh… no." The windows were starting to fog up, so she wiped a spot to see through. "It's some white car. Stopped. Just sitting there."

"Lock your doors. Want me to hang up so you can call 911?"

"And say what? 'Hi, there's a vehicle parked in my personal space'?"

"How about, 'I'm a woman, all alone. My car broke down and now a strange car pulled over in front of me'."

Leslie shivered. *Because I'm soaked or scared?* "Stop it. You're making me nervous with your flair for drama."

"Look, this is no time for—"

"Shh. The driver's door is opening. I see someone getting out… and standing there. This is really creepy."

Rachel's voice dropped to a whisper. "Is it a man or a woman?"

"Just a sec…"

The figure suddenly ran to her door and started banging on the window. A man's voice seemed to come from miles away. "Hey, are you okay in there?"

Rachel whispered to her. "What's going on?"

Leslie's mouth fell open. "I gotta go."

"What? No, tell me what's happening first."

"If I told you who was standing outside my window, I don't think you'd believe me."

The man kept pounding his hand against the glass. "Talk to me. Are you okay? Do you need help?"

"Who is it, Leslie?"

"You'd think I'm lying. I'll call you later."

***

Joe Rohrer pointed his Camaro convertible into the passing lane to get by the lumbering school van. The distant sky threatened nasty weather. Chancing a longer glance toward the horizon, a face slowly appeared. *Aubrey.* Even though time had passed, he couldn't get her out of his mind. *Can't believe she dumped me for Connor.* The man who held the title of Aubrey's husband was once his closest friend. And now? Joe was doing an effective job of avoiding both his ex-friend and the man's new wife.

A ring tone interrupted his thoughts. Joe glanced at the media center display. *Daisy.* Talk about a friend. He and Daisy had been there for each other through thick and thin. Before his eyes, Daisy's pretty face replaced the one in the distance. *Too bad she's married.* If he could only be lucky enough to find someone as pure and sweet as Daisy Elliot...

He depressed the button on the steering column and accepted the call. "Hello, Daisy. How was your day?"

Her normal giggle warmed him. "It was fine, but I'm glad it's over. You headed back?"

"That I am."

"Are you in PA or still in Jersey?"

Joe noticed the growing lights of a huge truck as it closed in on him. He maneuvered into the slow lane to give it berth. "I'm just east of Coatesville."

"You know, Jake and I were thinking about throwing some steaks on the grill. Want to join us?"

He took a swig of the bottled water sitting in the console. "Be delighted. What can I bring?"

"Just yourself. So, did you give any thought to finding a partner? You know, so we can finally have that foursome you keep teasing me about? Jake and I have been practicing in the back yard."

"Oh, you have? That's a surprise."

More giggling. "Somehow, I never thought chasing a little dimpled ball around a golf course would become so addictive."

The scent of fresh cut grass came to him. Warm breezes under a cloudless sky. He sighed. "I'm glad you liked your birthday present."

"Golf lessons were a terrific idea. Hey, I know you've been at the conference at Wildwood the last couple of days. I've got some bad news for you."

"What's that?"

"You know the new girl, Amber?"

Joe had to think hard before it came to him. "Doctor Abercrombie's nurse, right?"

"Yes, that's the one. She was assaulted last weekend."

Chills ran across his shoulders. "Assaulted? Is she okay?"

"Physically she's fine, except for the black eye. Mentally? She's still pretty shaken up."

"What happened?"

"Hold on." Joe could hear Daisy talking to her husband, telling him to grab another steak out of the freezer. "Sorry about that. Wanted to get your order in with the chef. Last weekend. Amber was heading upstate to visit family. Her tire blew so she pulled to the side of the road. She was on Interstate 80. A couple of minutes later, a pickup slanted over. The girl stepped out, hoping they'd change it for her."

"Oh, no. What happened next?"

"Two men got out. They robbed her. Took her purse and jewelry, including her engagement ring. She fought back and they smacked her around, tied her up and then locked her in the trunk. The State Police told her she was lucky that was all they did."

"Poor woman. I hate stories like that. Makes me wish I would have been there."

Daisy drew a short breath. "Why?"

"Because I would have stopped it. It makes me so mad hearing things like that." He could see the rain coming. "Looks like I'm about to drive into a storm. I'll grab a bottle of wine and see you guys in a little while."

"Okay. Drive safe. See you soon."

Joe shook his head. *Why do men have to treat women that way?* If Joe had been there, he'd have put an end to it. He couldn't understand the cruelty and violence that seemed to abound everywhere these days. A vision slowly formed, of him driving along a deserted highway and coming along two men smacking around a lady. Pulling over, he grabbed a club from his golf bag and made short work of the thugs. The damsel in distress reached for him, kissing his cheek as a reward. The face of the girl slowly materialized—Aubrey...

The first fat raindrops splattered hard against the glass. The bad weather was upon him. Shaking his head, Joe cleared the daydream from his mind.

After the way she'd broken up, over the phone no less, would he really come to her rescue if the situation presented itself?

That thought was on his mind as he continued to drive on the Lincoln Highway. In the distance, he noted a vehicle along the side of the road. Joe caught a brief glimpse of a figure standing, then running to enter the passenger door. His heart started pounding hard when he got close enough to read the letters across the back window—Lapp Interior Design. The memory of Daisy's story grew in his mind. *Aubrey might be in that vehicle. If I later find out she's been assaulted and I just drove by...* Joe pulled off the road. A battle raged between his mind and heart as to what he should do.

"Connor drives a pickup, so it's not him. Probably his sister, but what if it's Aubrey?" It was raining too hard to see anything. Joe turned on the four-way flashers, pocketed his key and exited the Camaro. He stood outside his door and tried to peer inside the black SUV. The deluge prevented detection of whomever was sitting inside. Finally, he ran to the vehicle and knocked on the window. "Hey, are you okay in there?"

There was no answer and he could only make out the outline of a person. *Suppose there's someone in the back, keeping her from answering?* Joe pounded on the window this time. "Talk to me. Are you okay? Do you need help?"

The door opened. It wasn't Aubrey, but instead it was Connor's sister, Leslie. She slid across the seat. "Come in out of the rain."

Joe jumped in, slamming the door behind him. "What's wrong?"

Her hair was soaked and hung limply across her shoulders. "George died."

Who's George? "I'm sorry to hear that. Did you just find out? Is that why you pulled over?"

The blue in her eyes seemed to glow in the darkening afternoon. She covered her mouth to hide her giggle. "No. George is my car. He quit moving and I'm stuck here, until a tow truck arrives." A single drop of water accumulated and gathered into a drip at the end of her nose. She wiped it away with the back of her hand. "So... what brings you to my car door on this miserable day?"

His hands were starting to shake, now that the coldness had settled in. "I was on my way back from a conference in Wildwood. I recognized the vehicle and wanted to make sure everything was okay."

His eyes dropped to her lips. She was smiling. Now that he thought back, every time he'd seen Leslie Lapp, there'd been a smile gracing her face. "A couple of minutes ago, my day was pretty crappy. But now, it's getting better by the second."

"Do you have a ride, I mean after the tow truck arrives?"

She was still smiling, though less than before. "I was kind of hoping to hitch a ride with them."

The blue in her eyes kind of reminded him of Daisy. A strange and exciting thought developed in his mind. "I'm headed in your direction. I wouldn't mind giving you a ride home, if that's okay?"

Leslie's smile increased. "I thought you'd never ask."

Chapter Two

June

Isaac Golden climbed out of his pickup, basking in the scent of a freshly cut hay field. Two young women in long, black skirts and white bonnets wheeled past him on bicycles. One turned her head and nodded at him. The ladies slipped their bikes into a rack before entering one of the buildings. Isaac walked into the "main office," as the sign outside was marked. No one was visible, but noise from the back room told Isaac he wasn't alone. He calmly waited.

A tall man with reddish-brown hair strolled into the room from the back. Isaac stood and greeted him. "Good morning, Mr. Campbell. Reporting for duty, sir."

"Isaac, isn't it a beautiful morning outside? So good to see you." The man had a British accent. "And please, it's Henry, not Mr. Campbell."

"Sorry sir, old habits are hard to break."

Henry's smile put him at ease. "I know. I was also a Marine, though I served Her Majesty, not

Uncle Sam. Want a cup of tea or coffee while we wait for Edmund?"

"Edmund?"

"Yes. He's my younger brother and runs the day-to-day operations."

The front door swung open and a pretty black-haired lady entered. She was wearing shorts and a flowered top. The hint of apricots surrounded her, as did the aura of elegance and joy. When the lady offered him a smile, he noted two dimples, one on her cheek and another on her chin. Isaac also noted Henry's reaction—his eyes widened and a mile-wide grin split his face.

Before Isaac could think of something to say, the red-haired man did. "Ellie, aren't you the vision of loveliness this morning?" His boss strode forward and kissed the woman's hand. "Let me introduce you to the new mechanic I hired." The two turned to face him. "This is Isaac Golden. He just moved here from Minnesota and was a Marine. Isaac, this is my bride, Ellie Campbell."

The woman extended her hand. "Pleased to meet you, Isaac." She then turned to Henry. "I know you're busy and I'm sorry to interrupt. You forgot this and I could feel you might need it." She handed the man a cell phone. "I've got to get back to the kids. Can't wait to see you at lunch." The two kissed and she departed.

Sound in the back room again drew his attention. A shorter version of Henry walked through the door. "Morning, Henry." The man nodded at Isaac. "Hello. Are you the new hire?"

Henry answered. "Edmund, this is Isaac Golden, and yes, he's the mechanic I hired. Isaac, my brother Edmund."

Edmund extended his hand. "Welcome aboard. Mechanic, huh?"

Isaac nodded. "Yes, sir. In my last job, I repaired farm equipment."

"Great. We're glad to have you aboard. Why don't you come with me and I'll show you around. And Isaac?"

The faint scent of black licorice surrounded the short man. "Yes, sir?"

"I'm not a noble. Please don't call me 'sir'. I'm simply Edmund. Let's grab a cup of coffee before we start the day. Might need it because you never know what's going to happen next around here."

The door flew open and one of the young women he'd seen earlier rushed in. It was the one who had nodded at him. Even though she spoke to Edmund, her eyes were on Isaac. "Come quick. Mrs. Miller's cows are out again and they're in the sweet corn."

Edmund rolled his eyes and laughed. He winked at Isaac. "See what I mean? It's always an adventure."

***

Rachel Domitar walked up to the screen door of the old farmhouse. Hanging baskets of yellow and pink wave petunias spilled out of their containers on both sides of the frame. They seemed to be the welcoming committee to the home of her friend, Aubrey Lapp.

She raised her hand to knock but didn't get the chance. The door flew open and a short brunette lunged at her. "Aunt Rach!"

Rachel held the little girl tightly. "Grey, I missed you. Look at how tall you're getting."

"Thanks. Momma's out back. Come in."

The pair walked through the house and out of the kitchen door. Her friend was seated under an arbor shaded by trumpet vines, drinking iced tea. Dressed in white maternity shorts and a lavender top, Aubrey's eyes curved as a smile filled her face. "Hey Rach, so good to see you." Aubrey struggled to her feet.

"There's the dairy princess. Oh my, you're really getting big, but you have such a glow about you. How long do you have yet?"

Aubrey hugged her. "Six weeks to go. I'm happy to be a mom, but looking forward to getting past the pregnancy part."

Grey tugged on her arm. "We're having a little brother."

Rachel hadn't known the sex of the baby. "When did you find out?"

Aubrey grimaced as she sat down. "Our curiosity got the better of us, so we found out last week."

Grey's head was bouncing up and down. "And I got to come along."

The child was so adorable. "You did?"

"Uh-huh. My brother really likes to kick Momma."

Aubrey chuckled. "That he does."

"Well, look who it is. Rachel Domitar."

All heads turned to find Aubrey's mother-in-law standing there. The older woman walked over and then hugged Rachel. Though her real name was Mary, she preferred to go by the name Grey had given her. "So good to see you, Mimes. I didn't know you'd be here."

"I just stopped by for Grey. We're going to pick up a package."

"For my baby brother," Grey added.

After they departed, Aubrey poured Rachel a glass of tea and the two women sat across from each other. "You look so happy, Abs. I guess you love living here, don't you?"

"It's Paradise, you know?" They both smiled over the play on words. "I believe you'll feel the same way, soon. I'm so happy you're moving in with Leslie. I missed our friendship."

A swift movement above Aubrey's head drew her attention. A small, fast moving object was flitting between the red, orange and yellow flowers. "Is that a hummingbird?"

"Sure is. Usually there's two of them. So, did you start to move in?"

"No, but I will. As soon as Leslie gets home. The Civic's full. My furniture should arrive tomorrow. Would you and Connor mind lending a hand to unpack? Leslie said she should be home in about two hours. Care if I crash here until then?"

Aubrey laughed. "No, you're always welcome. Connor and Grey wouldn't mind helping, I'm sure. Maybe I can supervise or be the water girl."

Rachel's eyes focused on Aubrey's belly. "Sorry about that. Wasn't thinking clearly." She studied her friend's smiling face. "I'm really scared."

"Of what?"

"Did I make the right choice? I mean, I've always lived in Jersey, but I find myself moving to someplace new, so far away from the life I knew."

"Rach..."

She wrung her hands and looked down. "I've lost or given up everything I've ever known. I have no idea where the nearest store is, how to find the bathroom in the dark or even where to look for a job. I'm terrified I made the wrong decision moving here. It's so scary."

Aubrey struggled from her seat to wrap her arms around Rachel. "It will all work out, you'll see. Remember what you said when I came here to stay? You told me God had things planned and in order. And I know God never gives you more than you can handle."

Rachel wiped her hand across her cheeks. "I think He overestimates me and what I can manage sometimes. I left everything behind to come here."

Aubrey's eyes were smiling at her. "Not everything. Now you're in the company of people who love you. People who'll always have your back." Aubrey laughed.

"What's so funny?"

"I'm just thinking back to a couple of years ago. It seems we had this same conversation about me moving here, but now the roles are reversed."

Rachel's mind drifted back in time. Aubrey had suffered two broken legs in an accident and was so depressed. Rachel had arranged for her to move in with Leslie because her house was set up for a wheelchair. Little had she known Aubrey would fall in love and marry Leslie's brother, Connor. "That was different. I mean, you turned out to be the dairy princess. And you found paradise."

Aubrey's giggle continued at the inside joke. "You never know what God has planned. I'm thinking it's something good. Something very, very good. Just wait and see."

A deep voice interrupted them. "Hey, Aubrey. Would you like me to... Whoa. Didn't know you had company."

Rachel turned her head and drank in the man standing before her. Dressed in jeans and a tee shirt that couldn't hide his bulging biceps, the man sported a Vikings ball cap and a United States Marine Corps tattoo on his right arm.

His eyes locked on Rachel. He quickly removed his head covering and nodded at her. "Ma'am."

"Rachel, this is my brother, Isaac. He also just moved here, from Minnesota a couple of days ago. Isaac, meet my good friend Rachel Domitar."

He extended his hand. Rachel took it, noting the callouses, the warmth, the strength and how it made her knees weak. "Pleased to meet you. I'm moving in next door, with Connor's sister. You can call me Rach, but only if you'd like."

A smile spread across his face. "Rach? That's a cool name. Know what? You can call me Devo. That's what all my closest friends know me as."

Aubrey raised her eyebrows. "Devo? I didn't know that was your nickname."

He answered his sister, but his eyes never left Rachel's face. "Yeah. It's short for devoted."

***

Isaac held the little girl's hand as they walked the short distance to the home of Aubrey's sister-in-law. She wanted to walk instead of ride with her adopted parents. Grey looked up at him. "I heard Aunt Rach call you Devo. Can I?"

He was amused with this wiggly and giggly child. "Can you what?"

Grey wrinkled her nose. "Call you Devo?"

"Well, I don't know. That's usually reserved for close friends. Hmm... do you think we're close friends?"

Ever since he'd moved in, the girl hung around him, constantly asking him to play games. And she was good at them. "Duh. Don't you think so?"

"I certainly do. And since you let me call you Grey, I think that'd be just fine."

Her smile was ear to ear. "Can we skip, Uncle Devo?"

He couldn't contain the laugh he held inside. "Why not?" And so, the two of them skipped along the road.

Grey was singing a song and Isaac missed the sound of the bicycle behind him. His peripheral vision caught a glimpse of the young woman as she rode past. It was Rebecca Stoltzfus, who was both his neighbor and co-worker.

"You skip pretty gut for an Englishman." The Amish girl nodded and swept on past.

He yelled at the fleeting figure. "I'm not English. I'm an American."

The woman glanced over her shoulder and called out, "You're English to me, Isaac Golden."

28

Grey squeezed his hand. "That means you're not Amish. I think she likes you."

"Yeah. What's not to like?" His mind really wasn't on Rebecca or even Grey. Instead, it was on the lady he'd been introduced to earlier—Rachel. Her hair had been kind of messed up or maybe it was just the way she wore it. It didn't matter. He liked it. She'd seemed a little sad, at first, but when she looked at him, it was like a drop of happiness had reached her heart. For the first time in a long time, Isaac felt something start to warm inside him.

"Did'ya meet Aunt Leslie yet?"

"I can't say that I have. What's she like?"

"She's funny. Uncle Connie and her always pick on each other."

"Uncle Connie? Do you mean Connor?"

"Yep. She calls him that to tease him."

He liked Connor's sense of humor. "Sounds like a nice lady."

"Here's her house."

Isaac studied the yellow building with the green shutters and the long handicap ramp that ran from the drive to the porch. Pennsylvania was so different than Minnesota, especially the people. Back home, one didn't experience the immediate sense of friendship everyone here seemed to offer. In Minnesota, you had to know people for a long time before ever considering friendship.

"Do you mind giving me a hand with this box, *Devo*?" Rachel stood before him, trying to lift a large box out of her Honda.

"No problem, *Rach*." The smile the girl gave him lifted his spirit.

"Want to follow me?"

"Sure." *To the end of the earth?*

Grey skipped ahead into the house. Isaac hoisted the heavy box and followed the girl with the messy hair. "What in the world do you have in here? Your anvil collection?"

Rachel giggled. "Just my shoes."

"I have like... two pair of shoes to my name. How many did you stuff in here?"

Another woman's voice answered. "A girl can never have too many shoes." He turned to the voice and was met with a wide smile and a set of the bluest eyes he'd ever seen. His mouth was unexpectedly dry. "Who are you, by the way? I'm Leslie Lapp." She offered her hand.

Isaac stopped, balanced the box on his left knee and reached to meet her grip. Her touch set off a pleasant reaction against his skin. Isaac was suddenly at a loss for words as he memorized every feature in the woman's face. He simply nodded.

The woman named Leslie laughed. "You do speak, don't you?"

"Uh, yeah, sorry. I'm Leslie, no, I mean, I'm Isaac Golden. But please call me Devo. It's short for devoted."

"Devoted? To what?" Despite the smile on her face, Isaac felt exposed... naked.

He swallowed hard. *Don't come on too strong.* "Devoted to God, family and the Corps. In that order."

She placed a finger against her chin as she stared at him. "That's right. Aubrey said her brother was moving in with her. Must be you."

Connor, Aubrey's husband peered through the door. "That's him. If you were around more often, you'd know these things. Where *do* you go all the time, the world wonders?"

She turned and Isaac couldn't help but smile at the playful banter. "Wow. A university grad quoting not only history, but literature? I'm impressed. Look at you, citing both Nimitz's message to Halsey about task force thirty-four and the Charge of the Light Brigade? Did you read that in one of the comic books they gave you at Millersville?"

Connor nodded at Isaac. "You have to watch my sister. She gets easily confused. Leslie's remembering her days from college. Textbooks there had lots of pictures and small words." He turned to his sister. "Seriously, we miss you. Seems like you're never home. Where are you spending your time these days?"

Leslie watched her brother, and Isaac could see the corners of her lips curl. "I've been busy hiding from my over-protective, nosy and intrusive brother."

Isaac scratched his head. "Do you two like each other?"

Leslie rolled her eyes. "Since he's my *only* brother, I guess he's my favorite one." She patted Isaac's shoulder. "Just speak slowly when you talk to him. Connor's not the brightest crayon in the light bulb box."

"Hey, crayons aren't in a light bulb box."

"My point exactly."

Connor laughed. "Despite the evil attitude toward her loving brother, Leslie's okay. And don't worry. You'll grow to love her."

Both of the siblings turned and walked into the house. Isaac swallowed hard and then muttered. "I think I already do."

***

Joe Rohrer shook his head. He whispered to the Elliots, "She'll never make that shot. It's at least a thirty-foot putt."

Leslie pinched a few blades of grass, and then dropped them. "You do realize I can hear every word you're saying? Since you have such minimal little faith in my ability, why don't we make a little wager, *Joey*?"

Daisy clamped her hand across her mouth, apparently to contain her laughter. She turned to her husband, Jake. "Joey? She called him 'Joey'?"

Joe shook his head. "That's okay. My nickname for her is 'Lola'. She only does this type of thing to get under my skin, especially when there's an audience around."

Jake chimed in. "Joe, know what? I'll bet you a twenty Lola *does* make the putt."

"Okay, Jake, you traitor. You have a bet. She's gonna blow it."

Leslie knelt down to eye up the shot. "Why do you have such little faith in me, Joey? Wanna put your money where your mouth is?"

If she makes it, I'll end up regretting this. He nodded his head at Leslie. "Okay, smart aleck. Show us what you got."

She met his eyes. That perpetual smile creased her face and made her adorable. "What about you and me? Loser buys dinner?"

"Fine."

Leslie's blue eyes widened. "For everyone?"

"You're going to regret that, Lola. We have ourselves a deal!"

The blue-eyed brunette winked at him. "Here we go, Joey-baby." Leslie took one last look at the hole. As soon as the club met the ball, the dimpled spheroid arced to the left.

Miss. Miss. Miss! But Joe's mouth dried as the trajectory changed, almost as if an invisible magnet attracted the ball to the hole. *Plink!* It fell into the target.

Leslie breathed on her fingernails and then polished them on her shirt. "Daisy, how about dinner at the Stockyard Inn? Joey's buying, by the way."

Daisy fought to contain her smile. "Sounds good to me. I heard they have a forty-eight-ounce filet mignon."

Jake had a big smile as he stood next to Joe, hand extended. Joe opened his wallet and handed over a Jackson. "We'll go open your tab at the Stockyard. Daisy loves their fifteen-dollar margaritas. See you guys soon."

Leslie dropped her club into her golf bag, then walked until she faced Joe. "I'm an expensive date, huh?"

His arms found their way around her waist and he pulled her to him. Joe softly kissed those desirable lips. "Yes, but you're worth it."

Her eyes searched his. "Next time, maybe we can raise the stakes?"

His arms trembled in anticipation as he fantasized the possibilities in his mind. His words were barely a whisper. "What do you have in mind?"

Leslie swallowed hard and her smile dissipated. "It's difficult keeping our relationship a secret. I want to tell my family all about us. That I met the man of my dreams and how we're deeply in love. Maybe we can have a cookout and spring it on them, as a surprise. They'll love you. I promise. What do you think?" Her lips curled.

So much for my fantasy. The thought of Aubrey being there ruined it. "Leslie, I don't know."

His girlfriend's smile faded and she looked away. "I understand."

Idiot! Keep this up and you'll lose her, too. He touched her chin and moved her head until their eyes met. "It's really important to you, isn't it?"

"Joe, I love you, but hiding our bond from my family is becoming increasingly more difficult by the day. I believe they sense I'm lying to them. Even though we're not doing anything wrong, I feel... what's the word? Cheap."

He was silent as he gazed into her eyes. *I don't want that*. "Okay, but I'll need your help. Connor and I haven't spoken in almost two years."

Her blue eyes suddenly sparkled. "Maybe it's time for both of you to bury the hatchet."

He swallowed hard. "Okay. I'll do it, for you." *I just hope Connor doesn't want to plant it in my skull.*

Chapter Three

July

The coolness of the metal frame of the door was a sharp contrast to the heat on the porch. The pleasant scent of honeysuckle hung in the air. Leslie carried the plate of hamburgers to the grill. But the thought of food didn't do much for her right now. Not the way her stomach was rolling or hands shaking. *Help me calm down, please?*

"Anything I can do?"

Leslie turned to the girl sitting in one of the loungers. "Any good at mixing stiff drinks?"

Rachel snickered as she shook her head. "I've never seen you imbibe anything but an occasional glass of wine, since college, that is. Why are you so nervous?"

"Because... Suppose my family doesn't like him?"

"We all love you, Leslie." Rachel stood and gave her a hug. "Everyone wants you to be happy, even Connor, though I'm sure he'll tease you to no end. Why are you so worried?"

"You don't understand."

"Try me."

Leslie gripped the back of the chair. "This is so hard."

"Your boyfriend can't be that bad, can he?"

"Not in my eyes. But I'm afraid Connor and Aubrey will be upset."

A confused look covered Rachel's face. "What? Why would they both be upset?"

The sound of tires on stone briefly interrupted them. Connor and Aubrey had arrived. Leslie swallowed hard. "You'll understand shortly."

Connor scampered around the mini-van and helped Aubrey climb out. Her sister-in-law was petite, and the size of her belly seemed unjustly large. Aubrey's face lit up when she caught sight of Rachel and Leslie. "Hi, guys. Boy, this takes me back."

Leslie was curious. "To what?"

"To the Labor Day picnic, remember? A couple years ago. I was in that dratted wheelchair. Seeing how you've got all this food prepared, it reminds me of that day."

Leslie couldn't help but smile. "Yeah, I remember." That was the day she'd first met Joe. When Connor's long-term girlfriend had thrown a fit and her brother had bailed on them. But then, her brother's best friend Joe Rohrer parked his car in her drive. Connor had previously invited him and Joe arrived early. The man had been so eager to help. *I remember the first time I saw you, Joe. I was so attracted to you.* But Joe had been taken with Aubrey. He'd hung around with her instead of spending time with Leslie.

"You okay, sis?"

Leslie shook her head to break the trance. Connor stood before her. "Just a little nervous, that's all." She forced herself to smile, then hugged her sister-in-law.

"Why? Are you afraid I'll show up your boy-toy?"

For the first time she could remember, Leslie wasn't in the mood to tease or be teased. "Just be nice to him, okay?"

Connor backed away. "You look like you've seen a ghost. What's going on?"

Leslie looked away. "Nothing."

"Hi, everybody." Everyone rotated to see the owner of the voice—Mimes. She was holding Grey's hand. Isaac Golden stood behind them. They must have walked from Connor's house. Mimes's brows creased. "Leslie, your face is bright red. Are you feeling sick?"

Leslie could feel her face heat even warmer. "Why does everybody think something's wrong with me?"

Connor interjected. "There's not enough hours in a day to list all that's wrong with you."

After giving her husband the stink eye, Aubrey spoke. "You just don't seem to be yourself today."

"Why would you say that?"

The pregnant woman waddled over and touched her face. "In the two years I've known you, this is the longest period of time you haven't cracked a smile. That's not like you."

Leslie didn't quite know what to say. But Rachel answered for her. "I know what's bothering her. Leslie's afraid you won't like her boyfriend."

Leslie whipped around to face her. "Rachel Domitar!"

Rachel appeared not to have heard. "That you won't support her choice."

"Stop it!"

"That we won't be here for her."

Leslie felt naked, her thoughts and fears now visible for the entire world to see.

"But she's wrong, isn't she?" Rachel was looking at Leslie's brother.

Connor took a step closer. "You know Aubrey and I—change that, all of us—will always have your back, no matter what. Come on. We love you. You do know that, don't you?" He opened his arms. Leslie stepped into his embrace. Grey was the first to rush to Leslie but certainly not the last. Her family engulfed her in a group hug.

The rumble of tires on the stone drive captured their attention. As one, they all watched the white Camaro convertible roll to a stop. A man all of them knew, except for Isaac, stepped out.

Leslie concentrated on Connor's face and saw his eyes narrow. Her brother's lips formed a thin white line before he spoke. "What is *that loser* doing here?"

Swallowing hard before she spoke, Leslie answered. "Everyone, this is my boyfriend, the man I love. Joe Rohrer."

***

The group moved away from Leslie as Joe approached. Rachel could almost feel the tension. Isaac sidestepped until he stood next to Rachel. His voice was low. "Why does everyone look so upset? Check out how red Connor's face is. And who's that guy with the sports car?"

Rachel kept her voice low. "That man used to be Connor's best friend. His name is Joe Rohrer."

"Used to be? What happened?"

She turned to study Isaac's face. "Joe and Aubrey were an item."

His eyebrows raised. "What? My sister told me she fell in love with Connor the day they met."

Rachel shooed away a fly. "She did, but Connor made a mistake and drove a wedge between them. Joe just happened to be there and, well... he caught your sister on the rebound."

"Did Aubrey love him?"

"Yeah. I'm pretty sure she was in love with Joe."

Isaac removed his hat and scratched his head. "Then how'd she end up back with Connor?"

"Let's just say God brought them back together and she ended up saving—"

Mimes's voice interrupted their conversation. "Well, if it isn't Joe Rohrer. How are you today?" She extended her hand in his direction.

Rachel noted the pallor of Joe's face as he shook Leslie's mother's hand. "Good to see you again, Mrs. Lapp."

The older woman patted his arm. "It's Mimes. Mrs. Lapp was my mother-in-law."

Color started to seep back into his face. "Nice to see you again, *Mimes*."

He turned to the child standing next to Leslie's mom. "And look at you, Grey. You're so tall now."

The girl spun around. "Yep. I'm fast, too. Watch me run. See?" Grey started tearing around the yard.

Joe turned his attention to Connor. Everyone grew quiet as the two men shuffled until they faced each other. Rachel could almost see the tension between them. *Like two gunslingers facing each other in a showdown at noon*. But who would draw first?

Connor took another step and made his move, extending his hand slowly. "Missed you, Joe." Even from a distance, Rachel could tell Joe's hand was trembling as he met Connor's grip.

"I missed you, too. All the time we spent on the tennis courts and golf course. But more than that, your friendship."

Connor shook his head and chuckled. "What you mean is you miss beating me... and me picking up the tab all the time. You always seemed to win."

Rohrer's expression changed and he turned his gaze to Aubrey. "I didn't win everything. Good afternoon, Mrs. Lapp."

It looked like Aubrey swallowed hard. "Mr. Rohrer."

He nodded at her protruding belly. "It appears congratulations are in order." Aubrey looked confused. Joe nodded at her mid-section. "You know, you're pregnant."

Leslie broke out laughing. Everyone turned to stare at her. It was Joe who finally broke the silence. "What's so funny?"

"I couldn't help thinking..." She wrapped her arms around her belly and continued to giggle.

Her boyfriend coaxed her. "Go on."

"It's good to see you making use of all those years in medical school. That was an astute diagnosis. Bet the dean of Purdue's School of Medicine is awfully proud of you."

Rachel turned to observe Joe's reaction. The man's face crinkled up and he joined Leslie's laughter. "You know, Lola, you're nuts."

Connor looked confused. "Lola?"

Joe patted his arm. "My nickname for your crazy sister."

Leslie quickly kissed him. "Yep. Crazy over you." She turned to Connor. "Remember all those years you lived with me and the thousands of meals I made? Today's your turn to start paying me back." Rachel noted the bewildered look on Connor's face. "Guess what? I'm going to let you cook. And, to make it easy on you, I have the burgers waiting for you by the grill."

Connor shook his head. "Did you see how she did that, Joe? Leslie is supposed to be hosting the party, yet she delegates the grunt work to someone else. One good thing about it... at least the food will be edible." Connor nodded in his sister's direction, but directed the words to her boyfriend. "Do you really know what you're getting here?"

Even from a distance, Rachel noted the joy in Joe's eyes as he held Leslie's hand. "Absolutely. I'm getting a cheeseburger. And in case you forgot my preferences, make mine medium-rare."

***

Kim Landis stepped out of the car. Even though the sun was about to set, he thought it was still quite warm. *Jenna's favorite time of night*—when the sun was having its last hurrah and the breathtaking beauty of dark purple or orange clouds said goodnight just before the first stars appeared.

He walked through the rows of headstones until he found hers. Wilted lilies were in a vase. *And they'd be from Sam.* "Sam, the man Jenna loved more than me." Her younger brother.

"Hi, sweetheart. It's such a beautiful night and I was thinking about you. I can't believe you've been gone so long." Kim wiped his hand through his hair. "I miss you so much." He sat down and crisscrossed his legs. The blades of grass tickled his legs below his shorts. Memories of her smile made his eyes blurry. "I thought in time the pain would lessen, but it kept increasing. I finally gave in and went to see a therapist."

Kim caught the last rays of the sun as it set behind a distant barn. It was just an illusion he knew, but Jenna's face appeared as a ghostly reflection in the polished stone. "It's been almost five years. The therapist told me it's time to move on." It hurt so much more to say it here, at her grave, than when he'd rehearsed it at home. *Feels like I'm betraying you.*

A soft flapping noise drew his attention. Glancing upwards, he caught a glimpse of a bat as it feasted on insects. He forced his attention back to Jenna's stone. "But please don't think I'll ever forget you. No way I could, even if I wanted to." Kim paused. "I ran into your brother, Sam, the other day. He walks with a cane these days, I guess because of the accident. He's married now, to some older woman. They have three kids. Imagine your brother, the baseball star, pushing a stroller. Hard to think of Sam as anything but a teenager." Another moment of silence. "Sam's over it. When he told me the baby's name, I knew he'd made peace from losing you."

Kim pulled some grass from the lawn and examined it. He had to wipe his cheeks. Sam had gone crazy after the accident that resulted in Jenna's death. Kim's breath came out in short, measured puffs. "Bet you're wondering why I'd say that." Kim searched the sky until he pinpointed the first star. "Your brother named his little girl Jenna—after you. So, I guess your spirit lives on. You used to tell me about Heaven and how our love would live on after we died. I, I want you to know I'll always love you." Kim was struggling to maintain his composure. "Bye, Jenna."

He sat in silence for quite a while before he stood to go. The man brushed some grass blades from his right knee, but stopped before doing the left one. Caught in his leg hair was a piece of clover. He gently picked it off and examined the leaf. It was a four-leaf clover. *Is this a sign?*

Standing at his car door, he cast a final glance at her gravestone. Kim drew a quick breath. Whether it was his mind playing tricks or a phenomenon of the dusk, he hadn't a clue. But for a brief second, he saw it plain as day. Kim closed his eyes tightly and when he reopened them, it was gone. His hands were shaking as he placed the key in the ignition. Driving off, he couldn't get the image out of his mind. The vision of Jenna standing there—waving goodbye. *Did I finally lose my mind?*

Chapter Four

Mid-August

T he sky opened up and rain bucketed down. Isaac walked to the timeclock. A few feet in front of him stood the girl wearing the black dress and white bonnet. His friend didn't look happy today. *Probably not looking forward to riding her bike home in the rain.* After clocking out, he caught up to her.

"Good afternoon, Rebecca. Looks like it will be a wet evening."

She sought his face. "Yes, it will be, Isaac Golden. But this is gut. We need the rain so the hay can grow more." Her normal smile was missing.

"Would you like a ride home?"

"No. It wouldn't be proper. I'm a single girl."

Aubrey had told him a little bit about the customs of his Amish neighbors. Like how unmarried couples only rode in open-topped buggies. "Sorry. Didn't mean to offend you. I was just trying to be friendly."

Rebecca's lips pursed as she studied his eyes. "Wish all English were as nice as you."

The tone of her words bothered him. Isaac glanced through the window toward the horizon. A sliver of blue was on the western sky. "If you won't let me give you a ride, maybe you could wait a few minutes. Looks like the storm may be passing."

She nodded, but now didn't meet his eyes. "Waiting a couple minutes might not hurt." She plopped into one of the chairs.

"Would you mind if I sat with you?"

"Why?"

"Because I'm your friend. And I'm concerned about you."

"Don't you be fretting over me, Mr. Golden. My problems are my own and not any of your business."

Despite her words, he seemed to sense she was comforted by his presence. "I understand, but sometimes just having a friend be with you is such a comfort."

"And you would know this how?"

Isaac glanced to the west. The blue sky was growing. "My best friend was Donnie, since we were kids. We did everything together. Even joined the Marines at the same time." The memory of that horrible day nagged at his mind. "He got shot, right in front of me. I risked my life to try and save him. Ended up getting wounded myself. Donnie died that day, on the ground, right next to me."

He jumped at the touch of her hand against his arm. "I'm sorry."

Isaac nodded. "Thanks. It was hard getting past that, but I had some great friends in the Corps. They helped me."

"I don't know what to say, except I'll pray for you. Prayers for peace."

"Prayer also makes a world of difference." The compassion in her eyes couldn't be missed. "I'll pray for you as well, Rebecca."

Just as she opened her mouth to say something, Rebecca's face turned pale and she looked down at the table. Isaac turned to catch the Fuhrman brothers as they entered the room. They too were seasonal help at Campbell Farms.

The eldest, Matt, walked over. "Hey, there's my little Becky. How ya doing, honey? Want a ride home with Tommy and me? We'll let you sit between us, real cozy like."

Rebecca's face turned even whiter. "No, thank you."

Tommy put his hand on her shoulder. "Must have heard you wrong. I thought for a second you said no."

Enough. Isaac stood and faced the pair. They both towered above him. "Do you boys speak English? I heard her loud and clear. The lady said *no.*"

Matt laughed and slapped Tommy's back. "A lady? She ain't no lady, she's Amish." Isaac noted how the man mispronounced the word so it had come out as "aim-ish."

You dare to insult my friend? "I don't appreciate your tone or your implications. Apologize to her, now."

Tommy pushed Matt out of the way so he could stand in front of Isaac. "Make me, you little punk."

Isaac shifted to a defensive position. "Gladly."

Before either Fuhrman brother could move, an accented voice broke the tension. "Break it up, boys.

47

You know, I believe Isaac was right. You *do* owe the lady an apology. I'd suggest you give it now."

All turned to find Henry Campbell standing there. Something about him made Isaac shudder. *Not a man I'd want mad at me.* Both Fuhrmans took a step back as Henry moved closer. "I'm waiting."

Matt quickly spoke. "Sorry, Becky."

The Scotsman's eyes narrowed. "Mind your manners. You call her Ms. Stoltzfus."

"Sorry, Ms. Stoltzfus." Matt stood directly behind Rebecca. Staring down at her.

Henry cocked his head. "Time to say ta-ta, Matt."

The Fuhrman brothers exchanged a look before heading to the door. Matt muttered, "Bye."

Henry followed them. "I'll walk you boys out, so I can make sure you find your pickup."

Rebecca turned to Isaac. "Thanks, for nothing. I asked you to mind your own business, but no. In the future, please stay out of mine, Isaac Golden." She walked out the door into the rain.

Isaac shook his head. *And watch bullies treat you that way?* "I don't think I can do that, Rebecca."

***

Rachel curled her legs beneath her and sipped the iced tea. Leslie plopped down next to her on the porch swing. The brunette handed her a bowl and a napkin. "Picked up some peaches on the way home. Knew you'd want one."

"Thanks. How come you're not over at Joe's tonight?"

Leslie's smile was wide. "He pulled the late shift, but I might go over later."

"You two, acting like teenagers." The scent of the peach reminded her of the pies her mom used to bake.

"I was too focused on my future to have time for a boyfriend in high school. I'm making up for lost time now."

Using her fingers, Rachel split the fruit open to remove the seed. "I'm happy for you. First Aubrey fell in love, and now you. Is that why they call this place Paradise?"

Leslie giggled. "We're better known for our earthy aromas than love."

Rachel shook her head. "If you're talking about the stench from the legendary Stoltzfus dairy barn next door, you've got it. Now, getting back to the topic at hand..."

Leslie wiped her mouth with the napkin. "Seems like you and Devo have something started."

"He is intriguing... and kind... and funny, but I'm not sure we have the same interests."

"Have you two gone out?"

"A few times. He likes to hike and go cycling. And he's fascinated with the big river."

Leslie leaned forward so the juice didn't land on her clothes. "Which one, the Susquehanna or the Conestoga?"

"The first one. Another thing he loves is antiques. Never buys anything, but he could spend weeks looking. He took me to some place called New Oxford, which had lots of antique shops. Just not my thing."

Leslie's eyes lit up. "New Oxford? I know it well. That's close to Gettysburg. I love going to those little shops. It's like taking a glimpse of yesterday."

Rachel smirked at her friend. "Better you than me, girl."

In the distance, she noted someone walking on the road. *Speak of the devil.* It was Devo. "Looks like your lawn boy's on his way."

Leslie wiped her hands and placed her empty dish on the porch floor. "That was nice of him to volunteer to cut my grass. Connor's always done it, but with the baby and Aubrey and Grey, Devo's been a godsend."

"It's not like I've spent a whole lot of time here, but your landscaping has never looked better."

Leslie's smile grew. "Yeah. It's strange. Almost like that man can read my mind. Every time I turn around, I find a new flower or lawn decoration. Ones I would pick. Seems to know my tastes exactly."

They watched him approach in silence. Devo stopped in front of the porch and tipped his hat. The sun glinted off his tanned and muscular arms. "Good evening, ladies. Are you enjoying this fine summer's twilight?"

It was Leslie who answered. "Yes, it's a nice night. What brings you here?"

Rachel noted a twinkle in the young man's eyes as he took them both in. "Your grass looks a little high, plus I met a few weeds out back the other day that dared me to stop them. I don't want them to get ahead of me. One thing the Marines taught me was that a good offensive always pays off."

Leslie's eyes crinkled as she smiled at him. "And here I thought they only taught you how to be offensive."

A wide smile broke across his face. "That, too. You sound like your brother, all talk, without any of the thinking."

Leslie ignored the jab. "Hmm, I thought you cut the grass two days ago. It's all suddenly clear to me. You're trying to rack up the tally on what I'm going to owe you." A giggle followed her comment. Rachel shook her head. *Leslie sure loves to tease people.*

The man wrinkled his nose. "Connor was right."

"About what?"

Devo laughed. "He said you never listen, at least to men. As I've mentioned before, I'm doing this as a favor, for a friend. Besides, I cut Connor's lawn for free."

Leslie continued the banter. "I'm wondering if you have an ulterior motive." She lightly jabbed her elbow into Rachel's ribs.

Rachel felt her face heat. *Leslie!*

He nodded and his eyes led the smile. "You figured me out. I just come so I can view the beautiful sights." He winked. "And I'm not talking about the flowers. But alas, I got work to do." He tipped his hat again. "Now if you ladies will excuse me, John and I are going to spend some quality time together."

John? Rachel glanced at Leslie, who seemed to be mesmerized with the man. "Who's John?"

"Why, John Deere, Leslie's garden tractor. Have a great evening." He turned and walked toward the old bank barn.

Leslie whispered to Rachel. "He is *hot*." Louder now, she called after him. "Semper Fi, Isaac."

Without turning around, he pumped his fist in the air. "Ooh-rah!"

He disappeared into the building. Leslie turned to her. "Wow. Maybe I should stay home more often. I don't think I've met a more attractive man since, since—"

"Since Joe?"

Leslie's face flushed. "Why yes, of course. So-o-o, how's the job hunt going?"

Why'd she change the subject so quickly? "I don't know. There's a couple of open teaching positions, but there aren't any drama positions. I guess I'm too specialized."

"You have theater experience. Given any thought to one of the local playhouses?"

Rachel glanced at the barn. Devo had backed the lawn tractor out of the building and raised the hood. It looked like he was checking the oil. "I didn't see anything I liked. Maybe I'll take a retail job for a while, until something appealing opens up. It stunk losing my job after all those years."

Leslie touched her hand. "Everything happens for a reason. I believe God has something special planned for you. Remember when Aubrey got hit by a truck?"

Rachel turned to face her. "Yes."

"That was all part of His plan, to bring Aubrey here. So she and my brother would fall in love."

"And what was the reason I lost my job?"

"Maybe to bring you here. To find happiness."

Sadness suddenly filled Rachel's chest. An errant sob escaped. "And why did I lose Eli? Was that part of His master plan, too?" She wiped her cheek.

Leslie wrapped her arms around her. "We don't always know what God has planned for us. You just have to have faith."

"That's easy for you to say. You've got the man of your dreams."

Leslie whispered in her ear. "It will happen. I feel it."

I wish I had your faith. "I hate being alone."

"You're never alone. We're here—Aubrey, Connor, Mimes and me."

Rachel jumped at the touch against her skin, from the man standing in front of her. Devo. "I'm here, too, and always will be, Rach."

***

Aubrey sat in the lounger, watching Cooper in the swing. Her infant son seemed to love being outdoors. The roses were in full bloom and their fragrance added to the joy in her world.

The sound of tires on stone caught her attention. *Connor's home already?* But instead, it was Isaac's truck. He disappeared into the house. She faintly caught the sound of a pop top being opened. Seconds later, her step-brother eased out of the kitchen, careful not to slam the screen door. He carried two cans of Diet Pepsi and offered one to her.

Aubrey kept her voice low. "Thanks for the drink and for dropping Grey off. She was looking forward to the sleepover with Missi. The Espenshades are nice people."

Isaac nodded. "Yeah. The mother, Hannah, sent along a bag of treats."

"She's a great baker."

"That's what her husband said—the best in the land and the prettiest, or so he claimed." The man grew quiet as he studied her.

"Something on your mind?"

"A couple of things, actually."

"Like what?"

"An apology, first off. When my dad married your mom, I was so bitter. Hated your mom, not because she wasn't nice, but because she was everything my mother wasn't."

"I'm sorry your mom passed away when you were young."

He lifted his hat and slicked back his hair. "I don't remember much about her, not the way my brothers do. Dad, being a preacher and stuff, tried to hide it from everyone. They said she had a drinking problem. Got drunk one night and wrapped a car around a tree. Didn't walk away that time."

Aubrey's eyes grew blurry when her own mother's face appeared before her. Isaac didn't seem to notice. "Then Dad married your mom. She tried so hard to love us, but we were always causing trouble, especially for her. When she passed away, I understood your pain. Sorry I never reached out to you."

"It's okay, Isaac. We were just kids."

He offered a sad smile. "I missed out."

"On what?"

"Spending time with you. Look at you now. Mother, wife, friend and world's best sister. I'm sorry. Hope you can forgive me."

She rubbed his arm. "It's okay. We all have regrets, but look at us now. Let's not focus on the past. Let's build a future."

His smile became playful. "You're something, sis." Then his expression changed again. "Can I ask a personal question?"

"Of course."

"I noticed how tense you are around Leslie's boyfriend. Rachel told me you once loved him."

It was really warm all of a sudden. "Where are you going with this?"

"Bear with me for a minute. You told me you fell in love with Connor the minute you met him. Is that true?"

Eerie feelings started up her spine. "Thought we agreed to leave the past behind. And why are you asking me these questions? There are some things I *will not* share with you."

He turned so he fully faced her. "I'm not trying to pry. I'm asking because I think you're super smart and I look up to you. I'm really looking for guidance."

"I'm confused. What do you want?"

"If you loved two men, how did you pick? What made up your mind?"

"I finally listened to my heart."

"Come again?"

"Okay. Don't spread this around, but yes, I was in love with both men. One was so romantic, and adorable, almost perfect. The other was flawed, made mistakes, but he was the one who set my heart on fire. It took a big nudge from God, but I finally listened to what my soul was saying. And that's when I made my choice."

Isaac bit his lip. "And this Rohrer guy had a hard time with it? That's why he's so distant with you. Am I right?"

"Yeah. Where did this come from?"

He looked away. "J-just curious."

It all came into focus. "You're in the same predicament as I was, aren't you?"

Isaac's face turned bright red. He faked a yawn and glanced at his watch. "Oh, look at the time. Gonna head in now. Need to be at work early. Night, sis." He leaned over and kissed her head.

"Isaac Golden, come back here. I was honest with you, now it's your turn."

His smile returned. "You always were easy to trick. Even as a kid."

"What? You're not going to answer me?"

His smile faded. "I need to answer that question for myself first. Have a pleasant evening."

Aubrey shook her head as he stepped through the door. It was plain he was talking about Rachel, but who was the other woman? As if in response, the mooing of a cow drifted through the warm night. *Rebecca Stoltzfus?* "But she's Amish."

Chapter Five

Early September

"I think we have a friend."

Rachel glanced up from her laptop. Leslie looked annoyed and if she hadn't been there in person, Rachel wouldn't have believed it. It took quite a bit to upset Leslie. "Friend?"

"Yep. Did you glance outside this morning?"

"Uh-uh. What's wrong?"

Leslie shook her head. "I heard a noise outside late last evening. I crawled out of bed and turned on the outside light. I was peeking out the side window when I heard a crash out front. Our garbage tote was knocked over. I'm wondering if the culprit was that coyote Connor saw earlier this year. They're scavengers, you know."

Rachel swallowed hard. "Coyote? What do you mean, a coyote? I thought they only lived out west or up north or somewhere besides here."

Leslie's face broke into a smile. "What's the matter, cupcake? Are you scared of a little puppy?"

"They are not puppies, they're vicious pack animals and deadly killers! Why'd you even tell me that? Now I'm scared to go outside."

Leslie continued to tease her. "Good thing we installed indoor plumbing last year, huh?" Her friend's eyes lit up. "Maybe you should call Devo. I'm sure he'd jump at the chance to come protect you... with his camo shorts and those thick muscular arms. No coyote or other animal stands a chance against a former Marine. And he's totally devoted. Isn't that what he said?"

"You know what, Leslie?" A ping from her laptop prevented Rachel from saying something she'd have to ask forgiveness for later. "You're saved by an email."

Leslie laughed. "I was just leaving anyway. I'm heading to Carlisle for a presentation. Have a great day."

"Yeah, you too."

Leslie hesitated at the door. Her voice was somber. "Can I ask a favor before I go?"

A tingling sensation ran across her shoulders. "Sure."

"We're friends, right?"

"Of course. Until the very end."

"Can you come over here, quietly, and bring your cell?"

Rachel picked it up and tiptoed to Leslie. "Okay. What's up?"

Leslie whispered to her. "I'm going out into the wilderness. If a pack of coyotes drag me off into the woods, will you cancel my appointments and notify my next of kin?" Leslie couldn't hold back and held her stomach as a loud guffaw erupted. She touched Rachel's cheek. "See ya tonight."

"Jerk. I thought you were serious. Bye."

Rachel entered the password for the screen saver. She was about to open the email when a howling noise startled her. Jumping to her feet, she caught a glimpse of Leslie running down the ramp to her new Chevy.

Exhaling loudly, Rachel brought up the email, from some woman named Kim Landis. The email title was "Do you teach drama?" As she read the body of the message, she was shocked. Supposedly, this Kim lady was the department chair for a local high school. The previous drama teacher had unexpectedly resigned and the district had an immediate opening. Kim had found her resume, saw the local address and wanted to talk.

"This seems too good to be true." Rachel read the email a second time. Either this was a very well-crafted hoax or her ship had come in. "Leslie wouldn't do this to tease me, would she?"

For the next hour, Rachel debated whether she should call the number listed in the letter or not. Her curiosity won out. Her whole body seemed to tremble as she punched in the digits. To Rachel's relief, an automated message came on, stating the name of the school and asking her to enter an extension. She did. Even more shocking was the voice on the message. *A man's voice?* "Hi, you've reached Kim Landis, department chair of the drama and communication department. I'm either teaching or away from my desk. Please leave a message with your number and I'll get back to you as soon as possible. Remember to support the arts and have a great day."

The machine beeped. "Uh hi, this is, um, Rachel. I'm calling about the email you sent. Yeah, I'm interested. Thanks." Click. *What is wrong with me? That would surely be a horrible first impression!* She must have sounded like an idiot. Then she cringed when she realized she hadn't left a call back number.

Her second message was not much better. "Hello, Mr. Landis. This is Rachel again. I forgot to leave your message, uh, I mean my number on your machine. I was just so shocked to find you are a man... I mean every Kim I've ever met has been female, well, except... You know what? I'll try this again. Please ignore this message. Uh, bye."

After disconnecting, she banged her head against the wall. Following an internal pep talk, Rachel tried once more. "Good morning, Mr. Landis. This is Rachel Domitar. I'm contacting you about the email you sent. Yes, I do teach drama. I would very much like to discuss the possibility of sharing this fine art with your students. Here's my number. I look forward to speaking with you. Have a wonderful day. And, oh, by the way, please don't judge me from the first two messages. I haven't had to look for a job for many years and, uh, I hope you consider the previous attempts as rehearsals. Bye now."

Rachel dropped her phone on the table and headed for the bathroom. "I'm such an idiot."

She was surfing the web about an hour later when a noise attracted her attention. *My cell?* She walked over and looked at the screen. It was a local number, but wasn't one she recognized. "Hello?"

She was greeted by laughter, a man's laughter, but no other words. She asked again. "Who is this?"

"Rachel Domitar?"

"This is she, and you are?"

"Kim Landis. I've got to tell you something. That was the most creative way to get an interview I've ever heard of. I'm hooked. So, would you like to set up a time to discuss the position?"

After she hung up, she pinched her arm. *Did that really happen?*

***

Joe Rohrer held the door for Leslie. Though it had been a while, he recognized the smiling blonde who came to seat them. "Nice to see you again, Joe." He'd forgotten she had a British accent. The lady turned her attention to Leslie. "Good afternoon and welcome to the Essence of Tuscany Tea Room. I'm Sophie Miller. Table for two?"

Joe answered. "Yes, please. Sophie, this is my girlfriend, Leslie Lapp."

The hostess's eyes widened. "Girlfriend? Congratulations, Mr. Rohrer. Is today a special occasion?"

Leslie answered. "No. We had a little wager from our tennis match and Joe lost. We had agreed the loser would have to find someplace romantic."

The woman laughed and winked at Leslie. "If that's the case, I've got just the table for the two of you."

She led them to a secluded corner of the restaurant. There was a private alcove that overlooked a beautiful garden with a gorgeous water feature. "Would this be all right?"

Joe nodded. "I think it's perfect." He held the chair for Leslie, then sat across from her. "What do you think of this place?"

Leslie reached for his hand. Hers were so warm. "I never knew this shop existed, and it's only a couple of miles from home. I'm glad I whupped you."

"You have to rub it in, don't you? Did you ever consider the possibility I might have thrown the match to let you win?"

Before she could answer, the server was there. She handed Leslie a beautiful floral arrangement. "I believe these are for you. They were delivered earlier. Are you ready to order?"

He glanced at his girl. There was wonder in her eyes. Joe answered for them. "Can you give us a few minutes?" The girl nodded and walked away.

"You, you had this all planned, didn't ya?"

"Well, since you are asking, I'll admit I did."

"Why?"

He shrugged his shoulders. "There's a few reasons. I imagine I don't say this enough, but I'm so glad you came into my life. I've shared the disappointments of my past with you. For the first time, I feel like I'm really living. I love you, Leslie."

She started to lean across the table and he met her halfway. Their lips blended together. He had no idea what fragrance she was wearing, but it reminded him of spring flowers. Finally pulling apart, they sat back down. "I feel the same way. Did you know this past Labor Day was a kind of anniversary for us? Three years ago, you walked into my life. And now? You're throwing tennis matches so you can wine and dine me."

He couldn't help but chuckle. "You are aware there's something wrong with you, aren't you?"

The devilment in her eyes was evident. "Of course. I'm dating you."

Time to ask. "In all seriousness, are you happy with our relationship?"

Her response was soft and lacked any indication of teasing. "Yes. For the first time in my life, I'm in love. With you."

His entire body tingled. "Are you ready to take it to the next level?"

Her smile, which was always attractive, drew him in. "What do you have in mind?"

Here goes. "Let's take a vacation together. How would you like to go on a cruise through the Panama Canal? Two weeks of no phone calls, no interruptions. Just you and me. We'd leave from Miami and end up in San Diego. What do you think?"

She was breathing hard. "After the disaster on my last cruise, I'm not sure I want to go to sea again."

"What happened?"

"I, uh, fell overboard."

"What?"

"It's a long story. I had too much to drink. I was angry and... let's just say... I made a serious mistake. It was my fault."

He held her hand. "Leslie, it won't happen again. I'll be there with you and protect you from anything. Trust me."

Leslie swallowed hard. "I do, with all my heart." She reached for him, hands trembling. "How much will the trip cost?"

"Nothing. This is my Christmas gift to you. I booked it last month."

Her mouth fell open. "You what?"

"That's right. We'll set sail December 10th and disembark on Christmas Eve. We can spend Christmas in California."

The color in Leslie's face turned pale. "We'd miss most of the holiday season. I could probably swing the days away from my business, but this is Cooper's first Christmas. Can we do it some other time?"

"Not really. This, it's a, a repositioning cruise. The particular itinerary is only offered once a year."

"But Joe... my family."

How can I say this without sounding selfish? "If this relationship is going to work, we'll both have to make sacrifices."

She cocked her head and watched him. Her blue eyes were flaming. "And what sacrifice have you made?"

Joe sighed. "It's no secret how I felt about Aubrey. And how much it hurt when she fell for your brother, my best friend. You asked me to act like nothing ever happened, to have a normalized relationship. Forgiving both of them was hard, but I did it for you. And I'd do it again—but only for you."

A smile slowly filled Leslie's face. "Thank you for that."

It was a little hard to breathe. "Leslie, a strong love is like a tall tree. For it to have a long life and grow, it's got to be flexible. It bends with both gentle winds and hurricanes." Joe raised her hand to his lips and kissed it. "If you really don't want to go, I can cancel, I guess."

Her blue eyes now seemed to glow and that smile was bigger than he could ever remember. "It'll be hard, but let's do it." She squeezed his hands tightly.

The server returned. "Are you ready to order? What would you like?"

Joe couldn't help but see the joy in Leslie's face. "I have everything I could ever want, right here in my hands."

***

Isaac hoisted the satchel of tools on his shoulder. This afternoon, Isaac was making his rounds through the hothouses, performing preventive maintenance on the water circulation systems. He was reaching for the knob when the door flew open. Rebecca Stoltzfus ran through it. Her attention was focused on where she came from, not where she was going. The woman plowed into him, head first. Her momentum knocked Isaac backwards. He landed hard, but when Rebecca landed on top of him, it forced the air from his chest.

The girl was breathing rapidly. "Isaac! Isaac Golden. I'm sorry. What are you doing here?"

A voice drew his attention. "Whoa. I *knew* you were that kind of girl, Becky. So, you do like English boys after all, huh? I know you'll like me."

Isaac glared at the man looking down on him—Matt Fuhrman.

Rebecca rolled to the side and tried to stand. The other man offered his hand, but the woman ignored it. Isaac shoved the tool satchel to the side and stood. She quickly moved behind him so Isaac was between her and the other male.

"What's going on here?" Isaac quickly drew his own conclusion.

Matt tried to sidestep to get past him and get at Rebecca. "Mind your business, boy."

Isaac grasped the man's shirt and shoved the bully backwards. "Leave her alone."

"Golden, please. This isn't your—"

"Sorry, Rebecca. I just made it my business. Did they touch you?"

Tom Fuhrman walked through the door. He held a hammer in his hand. "Keep sticking your nose where it don't belong and it's gonna get bloodied up. *Boy.*"

Boy? You'll need more than that hammer. "Is that an idle threat or do you have the backbone to try and back up your big mouth?"

The larger man took a step forward. Isaac quickly analyzed his enemies and created a plan. *First, take the weapon away from him and then—*

The touch of Rebecca's hand was a cool contrast to the heat of the anger flowing through his veins. Her voice was high. "Golden, walk away. Please?"

Tommy laughed. "Hey Matt, look at the little wimp. Has to have a woman save him from a butt whoopin'. He ain't nothing but a scared little coward."

Isaac's eyes narrowed. "I'm not scared of anything, especially bullies like you."

Rebecca squeezed his hand. "Isaac, don't do this. Come wid me. I need some air."

She continued to tug on his limb until he backed away from them.

Matt laughed. "Sissy. A real man wouldn't walk away."

Isaac hissed through clenched teeth. "Real men don't treat ladies like you two do. Tell you what, we'll continue this later."

"I won't hold my breath over that."

Rebecca tugged on him. "Golden? Listen to me, now."

Isaac faced them as he stepped backwards until there was enough distance to be sure the Fuhrmans couldn't easily jump him. When he turned, Rebecca quickly released his hand. "What happened back there? Why were you running?"

She kept her eyes pointed straight ahead. "They were just teasing me, and, and I got scared."

He grasped her elbow and spun Rebecca around so she faced him. "There's a difference between teasing and harassment. They need to stop messing around with you, now."

Shaking her head, she answered, "I don't want to cause no trouble."

"You're not. They're the ones causing the trouble. It needs to stop, right now. And I can put an end to it, this instant."

"Isaac, I need to forgive and pray for them."

"No. You need to put your foot down and tell them to quit it. I think you need to tell Henry Campbell what's going on. That man will squash it."

"No, no. It's not our way."

"Your way? Rebecca, that's enough. Either you talk to the Campbells or I'll fix this, my way."

"Your way?"

"I know how to make them stop."

The girl was shaking. "How would you do that? Talk sense into them?"

"I don't believe any amount of talk will get through to them. Their kind only understands one thing, and for them, it will need to be both physical and violent."

"You know as well as I do, those boys won't fight fair. I've heard them say they want to hurt you. I couldn't live with myself if they did."

He stood tall. "Them, hurt me? I don't believe you know what I did before I came here. I fought for this country. I was a Marine. And once a Marine, always a Marine."

"I don't follow you."

"Marines never lose, especially when we're standing up for the weak and vulnerable. And when the person you're protecting happens to be someone you care about a great deal, a Marine is relentless. We never quit, we never back down from a fight. We only win."

She grabbed both his hands and didn't let go. "No, there's got to be another way. Fighting isn't the answer."

The girl's hands were shaking, her face full of angst. "Fine. Let's try it your way. How about if you ask the Campbells to move you to another team?"

"Do you think they'll let me?"

Isaac squeezed her hands. "I won't let anyone treat you like those boys have been doing. Edmund and Henry will have to move you or else I'll intervene. And believe me, I'll teach the Fuhrmans a lesson they'll never forget."

Rebecca released his hands and wrapped her arms around herself. "I'm scared, Golden. You mean too much to me to allow you to get hurt. I'll, I'll go talk to Edmund. Now." She pivoted and took three steps before turning back to him. Her chin was trembling as she extended her hand. "I need your strength. Please come wid me, my friend."

***

Rachel opened the folder and leafed through the neatly typed papers. *So unprepared for this.* It had been like forever since she'd had a job interview. Thankfully both Aubrey and Leslie had worked with her, sharing their experiences and grilling her in mock interviews.

A girl with thick, blonde hair approached carrying a beautiful china cup. "Here's your tea. Just flag me down if you want a refill or need something else."

"Okay." Rachel watched the girl as she flitted to table after table. It was plain to see her happiness.

Rachel took note of the ring the girl wore on her left ring finger. *No wonder she's happy. She has a husband to share her life.*

A tinkling noise caught Rachel's attention. The door to the tea room opened and a man walked in. He spoke to the hostess and the lady led him to her table. The wire-rimmed glasses he sported covered intense steel-grey eyes. The dark, short beard was neatly trimmed and failed to hide his strong jawline.

"Are you Ms. Domitar?" The trance was broken when she realized he'd already extended his hand.

His grip was firm, but not overpowering. "Yes. Are you Mr. Landis?"

He sat in the chair across from her. "I am, but please call me Kim." The brilliance of his smile was accentuated by the dark facial hair. "Do you mind if I call you Rachel?"

"Please do."

The server approached him. "Hi, Mr. Landis. The usual?"

"Yes, Ashley. That would be great. Have any bear claws today?"

"As a matter of fact, we do."

Kim turned his attention to Rachel. "Would you like one? They're made locally and are quite tasty."

"Uh, sure."

The bright smile was back. "Please make it two, Ash." He turned his attention back to Rachel. "Your message, or should I say messages, made me laugh. Did you plan out that sequence to get my attention?"

Rachel's face heated. "Well, er, actually, no. You see it's been a long time since I've had to look for a job."

He nodded. "I saw on your resume you'd been with the same district for nine years. I'm sorry they eliminated the arts."

How did he know that? "Your email surprised me. How did you know I was a drama teacher?"

He paused as the girl dropped off his tea and their pastries. "I saw your profile on one of the online business platforms. Since you listed Lancaster as your region, I assumed you weren't teaching."

Kim's smile seemed to be hiding something, as if they were playing cards and he had four aces. "Why would you assume I wasn't teaching?"

He took a sip of the tea. "The drama community in Lancaster County is close knit. I'm pretty sure I can name every single drama teacher and coach in the county. And their kids' names."

"Fair enough. How did you know about the downsizing at my last job?"

"I googled you as well as the high school. There's actually quite a bit of information about you on the web. I think I read at least five human interest stories from newspapers touting how Rachel Domitar had made a difference in the lives of her students." Kim sipped his tea, but his eyes didn't leave hers. "The dream of every teacher is to make a positive influence on our students, but you've actually achieved that goal." He looked directly at her. "I guess I should just confess it right now."

His eyes searched hers, making it difficult to take a deep breath. "What confession?"

"I'm greedy. I want to sign you on before the other districts realize you're available. No offense, but after checking out your career, you're a bit of a legend."

Really? Rachel's face heated. "Thank you. Do you want to talk about the position you have open?"

The man laughed. "We have a good program, lots of talent and a great parent organization that always provides anything we ask for. I'd like to keep moving the program forward. For example, we have a great communication lab that is tech heavy. I'd like to see each of the kids either star in or produce a video as a senior project. There are four theaters in the area. I believe there's a partnership opportunity between our kids and the local venues."

"Wow. You have big dreams, Mr. Landis."

"Kim, please. So far that's all they are—dreams. We've been taking baby steps and my hope is the person we'll hire will make those dreams a reality. Help us build a legacy of greatness for the kids. From what I've read about you, I think you're just the one to lead us there. What are your thoughts?"

"I, uh, I'm a little, uh, wow. I don't know what to say."

"Sorry. My fiancée, well ex-fiancée, used to say I'm a man of intensity. I apologize if I came on too strong."

"No, no. You're fine. My ex-fiancé used to tease me about being a little slow on the uptake."

His eyes grew soft. "Sorry."

"For what?"

"About the ex-fiancé, but I guess we shouldn't talk about that."

Rachel sighed. "I agree we should let sleeping dogs lie."

The brilliant smile was back. "So, Rachel, where do you see yourself in ten years?"

***

Kim escorted Rachel to the parking lot. She climbed in a white Civic and he waved as she drove off. Turning his eyes toward the horizon, the distant hills were dark, yet the iridescent blue topping the distant vista gave life to the evening. *You would have loved the sky tonight, Jenna.*

Ashley and two of the other waitstaff headed to their cars. Kim and Rachel had closed the place down. A quick glance at his watch revealed the "interview" had lasted over four hours. He'd told her HR would be in contact. But even before meeting her in person, Kim had notified Human Resources to make an offer to Rachel.

There'd been a significance to the night and their talk. For the first time in half a decade, feelings that had died with Jenna were slowly creeping back into his chest. *Is it because she reminds me of Jenna?* Her fingernail polish was the exact shade his girl had worn. The kind of messy, kind of curly hairstyle was similar and oh so attractive. But the thing that almost drew him in, what made him will time to stop... it was her eyes. Rachel hadn't said a whole lot—change that, talked a lot. But her eyes had spoken volumes.

Kim suddenly noticed the moon. Just a crescent. He mulled the word "crescent" over in his mind. One of Jenna's dreams, on her bucket list, had been to ride the Crescent Limited rail from New York to New

Orleans. *Do you like trains, Rachel?* Somehow, he knew she loved them.

He'd talked too much, monopolizing the night. But Rachel's eyes had taken the time to whisper to him, confessing three things. First, those brown eyes tried, but failed to hide the pain. At the brief mention of her ex, pain had seeped out. *A lot like mine.* But behind the sadness, he'd caught a vision of something else. Whether it was her passion or the glimpse of the greatness she possessed, he wasn't sure. But it was there.

Kim swallowed hard as he remembered the third secret her eyes revealed. It had been just a slight shimmer, but he'd seen it. As plain as day. The revelation almost blew him away right then and there. Exactly what he wanted, no, what he needed in life. God had given him a wonderful peek into the future. And the thing that glinted in her eyes was... hope. Just waiting to get out, to laugh... to share... to dance... and to live again. *She's the one.*

The light was almost gone. As happened from time to time, Jenna's face appeared, this time in the orange and silver clouds. As he watched, a transformation took place. Jenna's face blurred and a new face appeared, but this time, the vision was crystal clear. It was Rachel's image.

Chapter Six

Late October

R achel plopped down at the table in her classroom. It was after school and she was famished. "That smells tasty."

Kim smiled as he opened the bag of Chinese take-out. "Here you go. Shrimp and cashews in lobster sauce with a spring roll."

A close friendship was developing between Rachel and Kim. It seemed he found a reason to hang around school every time she worked late. "What did you order?"

"Chicken lo mein and a shrimp roll. Want to try some?"

Rachel nodded. "Only if you'll have some of mine."

"Deal." She dished out a few bites of her combo onto his plate. He used chopsticks to share his dish. "So what do you think? Are we going to be able to pull this off?"

"We'd better." Kim was talking about their choice of a holiday play. She had proposed *It's a Wonderful Life*. And to her utter surprise, he'd agreed. "What you mentioned to me during our first meeting was the full truth."

His smile made her feel a little lightheaded.

Kim finished chewing his food before continuing. "Which part? About when I said how much of a legend you were and I wanted you for our school?"

Rachel's face warmed. He always seemed to find a way to compliment her. "No, the part about how talented the kids are, as well as the devotion of the parent organization. Did you know they've already supplied every single thing on my wish list? And most of the backdrops and scenery are ready, thanks to the parent volunteers. Unbelievable."

Kim slurped a long noodle. "You've created a lot of excitement in the district. This show is a major undertaking and your enthusiasm is contagious. Some of the kids in the cast were ones your predecessor tried to recruit, but they were never interested in performing. It's almost like you've brought some sort of magic to our school."

Another compliment. She knew her face was turning red. "You deserve a lot of the credit. You know, it's so refreshing having people support your ideas, without a million questions or inserting their suggestions on how to change things so they get the credit. Good people—like you. Thank you, Kim."

"You're welcome." It seemed as if he was going to say something, but instead he smiled slightly and engaged her eyes. And it was then that the world melted away. The only thing that really mattered was Kim. The depth of those steel-grey eyes was limited only by her imagination. And the longer the silence persisted, the quicker her heart pounded. *Is tonight the night he's going to ask me out?*

He finally inhaled sharply and shook his head. Kim picked up some more noodles with the chopsticks. "Why did you pick this particular show? I mean, I don't think any other district in the county ever put this one on."

"*Wonderful Life* has it all. Romance, nostalgia, humor, tragedy and a villain you love to hate. But the thing that draws me in is the internal struggle George Bailey goes through. All his life, George has had to sacrifice his dreams to help others. And, on Christmas Eve, when his uncle loses the money and Bailey searches for a way out... he doesn't seem to have a choice. George believes he's worth more dead than alive. He considers ending it all..." Immense sadness popped its head into her mind. The room became blurry and she had to stop.

The warmth of Kim's hand shocked her. His voice was soft. "Just like George Bailey, I've been there. I understand the hopelessness. For me, that moment was when Jenna died."

Kim looked so sad. Rachel had to stifle the desire to hug him. "Who was Jenna?"

The man sniffed hard. "My fiancée. Died in an auto accident, about five years ago. I was crushed. I felt as if I'd lost it all. Like there was no reason to live anymore."

"I'm sorry."

He wiped his cheeks and looked away. "Thanks."

Should I tell him? Her heart answered immediately. "Eli disappeared on our wedding day." Despite the years that had passed, the pain was almost as intense as the day it happened. Her jaw was trembling. "To this day, I don't even know for sure what happened. He said he was leaving and asked me if I would go with him. But when he told me I'd have to leave my family and friends behind and never contact them, again? I just couldn't do it."

Kim snugly gripped her hands. "Did he go into Witness Protection?"

Rachel fought back another sob. "I'm not really sure. All I know is all my dreams and happiness vanished with him. I've struggled with depression every day since."

He sniffed again. "Some pair we are, right?"

"Yeah, I guess so."

His eyes suddenly lit up. "May I share something with you?"

"Sure."

"This, this may not come out right, but I want to tell you something. The result of my soul-searching of the past five years has been this. Hope does exist. Hope of redemption. Hope of rebirth, of future happiness." He paused and his eyes probed hers. "Do you know how I came to that conclusion?"

Rachel was captivated by the look on Kim's face. "No. How?"

He hesitated longer, piquing her interest even further. "Because of you. The day we met, I saw something in your eyes." He watched her face, possibly for a reaction.

"Wh-what did you see?"

"Please don't think I'm crazy or being weird."

Then don't put it like that. "Okay. I'm listening... with an open mind."

"I saw the pain in your eyes when you mentioned your ex-fiancé, but I also recognized something else that was even more important."

"Really? What did you see?"

His gaze locked on hers. Drawing her into him. "I saw hope, no, not just hope—something even greater. Maybe it was desire, or possibly belief in the future. Belief that everything you'd lost would be restored, and, and..."

How can he know my exact thoughts? She continued his sentence. "And made not only whole, but replaced by something much greater, better, deeper and even more beautiful than what I lost." She shook her head. "I don't understand, Kim. How could you possibly know this?"

He swallowed hard. "Because those are my own exact thoughts, too. Something's happening between us, Rachel. It's almost like we're kindred spirits. Don't you see it? We were meant to be. Like we're two halves separately, but in reality, we're one."

Her chest suddenly tingled and her mouth went dry. "I, uh, don't know what to say."

Kim's face paled and he looked away. "Oh my God. I'm sorry. I got carried away and overstepped my boundaries. Years of loneliness must have made me see things that aren't there. I promise I'll never bring anything like this up again." He stood, prepared to go.

"Wait. I'm kind of in shock. Can we just slow down for a minute?"

"I never should have brought it up. I thought..." His voice trailed off.

Rachel touched his hand. "First things first. I don't understand this. I, uh, how could you know exactly how I feel inside? It's like you were reading my mind. How is this possible?"

"I'm not sure. Maybe it's fate."

"I'm beginning to think it's something more."

Kim looked confused. "Like what?"

Rachel smiled, with hope. "Maybe this is God's will."

***

Leslie took a break to admire the work. Her brother Connor was giving a hand decorating the bank barn in preparation for the big Halloween party. "I don't believe the decorations have ever been spookier. What do you think? Isn't this outstanding?"

"I guess it's okay."

What? "Okay genius, tell me what you'd do differently."

The blue in his eyes sparkled. *Here it comes.* The two of them had been teasing each other for as long as she could remember. He just stood there smiling at her. *Looking dumb.* "I'm waiting."

"I just think we could do better. And I have a suggestion on how to improve it."

"And that would be..."

"If you want to make it really, really scary, you should... hang up your picture. That will surely make the guests scream."

"Har-de-har-har. You know, I still have your seventh-grade class photo. Remember? Your hair was all matted down. And let's not forget your Tool

Time sweatshirt. By the way, if your wife hasn't seen it yet, I could order one so you could mount it over the fireplace." She yanked her phone from her pocket. "Oh, wait, here it is. Texting it to Aubrey now."

Her brother's mouth dropped open and he tried to grab the phone from her hand. She turned away and pretended to text. "You had that photo on your phone?"

I think I'm winning this one. "I keep it there for emergencies."

"I'm your favorite brother. You wouldn't do that to me, would you?"

"Aww. You're my only brother. Give me one good reason I should spare Aubrey from seeing this."

Connor's nostrils flared. "I didn't want to have to do this, but you leave me no choice. I'll show Joe the pictures of when you were in your Goth period."

"You wouldn't dare!"

"Try me."

They stared at each other for a good ten seconds before Leslie started to giggle. Connor joined her. "Okay, you win. Seriously, what do you think?"

"It's looking good, sis. I think if we hang a few more ghosts up there in the rafters and a couple more strands of lights... we'll be good." They shared a smile. "Thanks."

"For what?"

"For the wonderful memories and our closeness. For the traditions we've made. Ones we're passing on to Grey and Cooper and..." Leslie could see the sparkle in his eye, "...your children, someday."

The walls of the barn seemed to close in. *Need to tell him.* "Um, let's not rush things."

He laughed softly. "So the relationship with Joe is off limits for teasing? What's going on?"

Leslie swallowed hard. "We, uh, we've decided to take it to the next level."

Connor's eyes widened. "Did he propose to you?"

"No, no. Not that."

"Then what?"

"We're, like, going away on a mini-vacation... together."

Her brother took her hands. "I'm happy for you. Where are you going?"

"We're going on a cruise."

"Ooh. Pulling out all the stops. Cruise to where?"

"The Panama Canal."

"Impressive. So, tell me more."

Before she could say anything, the door to the barn opened. "Hello? Connor, are you in here?" Devo entered and quickly removed his cap. "Evening, Leslie."

Despite the chill in the air, the man only sported a long-sleeved shirt. *He even makes flannel look sexy.* "How are you?"

"I'm well." He turned to face her brother. Devo stood at attention and quickly saluted. "Sir. Message from your commanding officer, sir."

Connor's lips curled. "At ease. What's the communication from the general, sergeant?"

Leslie couldn't help but snicker at the banter. "Your commander ordered you to sneak behind enemy lines and raid their supply base." Devo handed Connor an envelope. "Here are your sealed orders, sir."

Connor slid his finger beneath the flap and liberated the contents. He smiled when he read it.

Leslie tried to grasp the paper from his hand, but her brother pocketed it. "Sorry. It's an eyes-only communique. I have to leave now. Can we finish the decorations tomorrow night?"

Joe and I have a date. "No, I'm busy. I'll just finish it myself."

The other man interjected. "I could lend a hand."

Leslie faced him. He was cute. And that shirt sure didn't hide his muscular arms. It was awful hot in the cold barn. "Thanks. That would be sweet."

Connor hugged Leslie. "Gotta go. See you in the morning." He scampered out of the door.

Leslie asked Devo, "What was that about?"

"Aubrey needed a few things from the store. I volunteered, but there must have been things on the list she didn't want me to see. That's why she put it in an envelope and licked it shut."

Leslie smiled. "You seem to fit in well with Aubrey and Connor."

A frown filled his face. "She's a great person. I regret not being there for her when we were kids. But maybe in time she and I will have a close relationship... you know, one like you and Connor do."

As Leslie watched his eyes, a vision entered her mind. Of Devo holding her close, as they watched the sun rise. His body was warm, arms strong, yet gentle. Then, his lips softly touched hers and they melted together...

"What can I do to help you?"

She mentally shook her head to interrupt the fantasy. "Uh, we, er, need to, um, put up a few more ghosts and more lights."

"Cool, I'll grab the ladder."

As they worked, they talked. Leslie couldn't help but laugh at his sense of humor. He told stories of some of the pranks he'd been involved with, as a youth and in the Marines. "Sounds like you have a good relationship with your brothers."

He tied off a loop of string so he could suspend a decoration. "Yeah, we're good. Had some rough times over the years, but we made it through. Now, we're close."

"So, why'd you move here? Lancaster is a long way from Minnesota."

Devo seemed to concentrate on making sure the decoration was perfectly situated. "I needed a fresh start."

"From what?"

He relocated the ladder and began to repeat the process. "Oh, I'm sure you know how it goes. Met a girl and fell in love. But she wasn't keen on staying faithful to me." He turned and engaged her eyes. "She broke my heart and nearly ruined me. It's a lot smaller community out there. Everyone knows your business. Got tired of the whispers." He shook his head. "A little tough, that's all."

"I'm sorry."

"I'm not. Everything happens for a reason. Now, God brought me here."

Everything happens for a reason? *I've been saying that for years.* "Well, I'm glad as well."

Devo shot a smile at her, which started melting her heart. "So, what's your story?"

"Wh-what do you mean?"

He climbed down and grabbed another decoration. "I was just thinking, a beautiful lady like you, great personality, smart... You are like... like the perfect woman. I'm sure you've had to fend off droves of men. Did someone hurt you?"

His compliment flustered her. "Hurt me?"

"I remember the night you introduced your boyfriend to the family. Aubrey told me that was the first time you'd been serious about anyone. I was just wondering if someone broke your heart."

Wow! He's thoughtful as well as cute. "No, nothing like that. I—it's just that I've always had this dream of being a successful business owner. I've put my heart and soul into the company and left romance on the back burner. Now, with Aubrey and Connor's help, I finally have some time for myself."

Devo threw the rope over the wood above him. "How long have you and the good doctor been dating?"

"Six months." She transferred another miniature ghost to him. "I think this is the last one."

He laughed. "Man or decoration?"

She joined him. "Decoration, silly."

"You sure? This is the most fun I've had since I've arrived in Lancaster."

She wrinkled her nose. "Hanging off a ladder and putting up fake ghosts is fun to you?"

Devo stored the ladder, then walked until they stood toe to toe. "That wasn't what I was talking about."

"Oh, then what did you mean?"

His eyes were so blue, his face so handsome. Devo's smile seemed to beckon to her. "Spending time with you."

**

Rachel stepped from her car and climbed the ramp to Leslie's porch. Despite the cold, she decided to linger for a while. The stars were brilliant this evening. Funny, all those years she lived in New Jersey, she'd been oblivious to the evening sky. *Am I always this ignorant to what's around me?*

A sliver of light and gentle laughter tugged her attention from the heavens. Joe and Leslie were standing outside the bank barn. *That's funny. I don't see Joe's car.* She watched as the pair shared a long hug. Then the taller shadow headed down the road, toward Aubrey's house. Rachel's mouth went dry. *Devo?*

The brilliance of the Milky Way was in no way as interesting as what she'd witnessed. Leslie had her back turned and was waving to the retreating figure. Rachel used the opportunity to sneak inside. Quickly positioning herself in front of the TV, she acted surprised when Leslie walked in. Her friend seemed startled when Rachel spoke. "Hey girl, how was your night?"

Leslie's face was flushed. "Good, good. The barn's ready for the party."

"Did you and Connor finish everything on your list?"

"Uh-huh."

"I didn't see his truck."

"He, uh, had to leave earlier. Aubrey needed something from the store and he skedaddled."

It was plain to see something had happened. Her face was still red and her eyes were distant. "You see a ghost or something?"

"What?"

"What happened after your brother left? Did you finish all by yourself?"

Leslie's right eyebrow arched. "You know, don't you?"

"Know what?"

"Devo came over to help."

"Oh, really? Did you two have fun?"

Leslie shook her head and stared out the window, toward the barn. "I can't believe this. What was I thinking?"

What did she do? Rachel forced herself to be calm. "What are you talking about?"

"Joe's a wonderful man. Handsome and kind. The type of man any girl would die for, right?"

"Yes. What happened?"

Leslie studied the floor, like a child who had to confess they'd done something wrong. "I kissed Devo."

Rachel's entire body tingled with surprise. "You what?"

"We had such a good time, talking and just having fun. And then when he said it, I couldn't help myself. I needed to feel his lips on mine."

"What did he say?"

"It wasn't really the words he said. It was the feeling behind them."

She'd never seen Leslie so flustered. "What exactly did he say?"

Leslie swallowed hard. "That spending time with me tonight was the best thing to happen to him since he arrived here."

"That was kind of him."

Leslie shook her head. "And then, and then, I could see it." She turned so the two of them could see each other's eyes clearly. "As plain as day, I saw the love in his eyes. Like I was looking into his heart. I was so stupid. I wrapped my arms around him and kissed him. Long and soft."

Rachel had suspected Devo was attracted to Leslie. "Wait. You kissed him or did he kiss you?"

"No, no. It was me. At least the first one was. After that, I'm not sure."

"Leslie! How many times did you two kiss?"

"I don't know, maybe a dozen... or two. He finally pushed me away and told me we had to stop."

What? "It sounded like a very passionate moment. Yet he wanted to stop?"

"Devo apologized and told me he wanted to respect the relationship I have with, uh, with uh..."

"Joe?"

"Yeah, Joe."

"I saw the long goodnight hug."

Leslie grabbed her arms. "Please don't tell anyone. I just, I don't know. Why did this happen? I love... love..."

Rachel was laughing. "Joe?"

"Yes! What do I do?"

"Why'd you kiss Devo?"

Leslie shrugged. "I have no idea. It defies logic. Joe's so handsome and Devo's cute, but there seemed to be some sort of magic tonight."

"There was definitely something strange about tonight. I'm not sure if it's the way the stars lined up or what. I had a shocking evening, too."

Leslie's eyes seemed to show concern. "What happened to you?"

"I've told you how attracted I am to Kim and I've been hoping he'd ask me out."

The color was beginning to return to normal in Leslie's face. "Go on."

"Well, we went from zero to sixty in a matter of seconds. We were talking about the play and well, next thing I know we started talking about feelings. Either that man has the ability to read my mind or, as he put it, we're 'kindred spirits'."

"And this happened tonight?"

"Yep. He told me we were meant to be together."

"Whoa, as in *you and him* together? Not just like, working together?"

"Uh-huh."

"And how do you feel about that?"

Rachel shook her head. "It happened so fast. I'm just not sure. I really, really like him, but I know so little about him, yet everything I see says he's a great man. But then this voice in my head reminds me, so was Eli."

"Oh, Rach." Leslie hugged her. "You can't live in the past. There's a reason for everything. Maybe God brought the two of you together for something special."

Rachel couldn't help it. She burst out loud with laughter.

Leslie looked confused. "What's so funny?"

"A reason for everything?"

"Yes. I firmly believe everything that happens is a part of God's greater plan."

Rachel sobered. The conviction of Leslie's belief was right before her. Rachel whispered to her. "Then why did God move you to kiss Devo?"

Chapter Seven

Mid-November

A ubrey noted Leslie's hands were shaking when she set the coffee cups on the table. Her sister-in-law also seemed pre-occupied. "You take it black, right?"

"Um-hmm." Aubrey wrapped her hands around the steaming cup of java. "It's been too long since you and I had a chance to just relax and enjoy each other's company. I miss that."

Leslie glanced out the window, obviously looking for something. "I am, too."

Where is her head? "Connor and I decided to relocate to Bolivia and join a commune."

"That's nice."

"Then we're going to raise rabbits, kohlrabi and kangaroos."

Leslie nodded and turned to Aubrey. A look of confusion spread across her face. "Wait. Did I hear you right? Did you say kangaroos? And what is kohlrabi? What are you talking about?"

Aubrey couldn't help but laugh. "What's going on with you?"

"I don't know what you mean. There's nothing going on."

"Sure, and the dairy farm down the road doesn't smell in the summer heat."

Leslie frowned. "Why do you think there's something wrong?"

The bitter taste of the coffee carried a trace of hazelnut. "Ever since the Halloween party, you haven't been yourself. You've been distracted."

Leslie walked to the window. "Don't know what you mean."

"Are you and Joe having problems?"

"No, no. Nothing like that. Joe's the perfect man." Her sister-in-law turned in her direction but didn't quite meet her eyes. "But I'm not telling you anything you don't know."

Leslie was referring to when Joe had dated Aubrey. She had loved Joe, but Aubrey had also fallen in love with Connor. It struck her. "Oh my gosh. Did you meet someone else?"

Leslie's face lost all color. "How can you tell?"

"Just the way you reminded me about what happened between Joe and me."

Noise started outside. It sounded like a leaf blower. Leslie peeked through the curtain. Aubrey stood so she could see who Leslie was staring at. *Isaac?* Aubrey shifted her gaze to Leslie. "It's my brother, isn't it?"

Leslie continued to watch through the window. "It's your fault, you know?"

"How is this my fault?"

"You sent Devo over to give Connor that shopping list the night we were decorating the barn."

"Okay."

"Your brother volunteered to stay after Connor left. While he worked, we talked. And when he said spending time with me was the best thing to happen to him since he came here, I think I misunderstood what he meant."

"I'm not following you."

Leslie finally directed her attention to Aubrey. "When I looked into his eyes, it was like, let's just say, it made me feel something I've never felt before."

"And then?"

"I kissed him. Not just once, but over and over again. I lost control and, if he hadn't stopped it, I'm pretty sure I can guess how the night would have ended. I've never wanted a man as badly as I did that night."

Aubrey touched her arm. "And this is what's bothering you?"

"Not exactly."

The older woman trained her attention to the man who was corralling the leaves. Aubrey waited until she continued. "He probably hates me... thinks I'm a tramp."

"Why would he think that?"

"Joe's my boyfriend. But I couldn't help myself. I'm the one who kissed him."

"Was it a thank you kiss or..."

Leslie seemed to fight back a sob. "No, definitely not just a thank you kiss. And I was helpless to stop myself."

"Why did he break it off?"

"To protect me. Your brother is an honorable man. He blamed himself for tempting me. Devo said he wanted to honor the relationship Joe and I have, and not drive a wedge between us."

"Okay, so you slipped up for a brief moment. Now what?"

"Nothing like this ever happened before. I mean, Joe was the first man I ever kissed. And then, then, I kissed Devo. And I've never done the things I wanted to do with Devo that night."

Aubrey swept Leslie's hair from her face. "Have you talked to Joe about this?"

Leslie jumped back. "Are you crazy? He'd dump me in a second."

"Okay, did you talk to Isaac?"

"Devo? No, he's ignoring me and I don't know why. Is it because he thought I acted like a tramp or because he just doesn't care about me? Maybe it was all in my mind."

Aubrey noted Leslie's limbs were trembling. "Do you care for him?"

She turned her head so she wasn't facing Aubrey. "I love Joe."

Aubrey placed her cup on the counter and touched Leslie's shoulder. Leslie turned into Aubrey's arms as the two hugged. "I didn't mean for this to happen. I don't comprehend why I kissed him. I cheated on Joe."

"No, you didn't. There was no commitment."

"Perhaps not a ring, but yes, there's a promise there."

"It was just a kiss."

Leslie shook her head. "It felt like a lot more."

"You really care for Isaac, don't you?"

"I told you I love Joe."

"But you're attracted to Isaac, aren't you?"

Leslie pulled out of the hug. Her gaze was focused on the floor when she nodded. "I'll admit I thought he was cute... and so polite." Leslie's eyes now engaged hers. "But then, when I saw it in his eyes..."

"Tell me. What did you see?"

Leslie swallowed hard. "Everything I've ever wanted."

***

Isaac threaded the plug into the oil pan. All he needed to do was refill the oil in the John Deere and then he was finished with the tractor.

The door to his shop swung open. Rebecca Stoltzfus walked in. She was carrying a basket. "Afternoon, Golden. How be you on this chilly afternoon?"

He couldn't help but smile. His Amish friend was always so kind to him. "I'm well, Rebecca. How about you and your family?"

"We be well. I brought you a little something." Rebecca lifted the cover off the basket and removed a large plate of golden cakes. "These are sugar cakes. I made them myself... just for you." Her face reddened considerably. "I hope you enjoy them."

He was touched. "They look delicious. Let me wash my hands, make us a cup of coffee and we'll have one together."

She glanced at the door. "Maybe, if we do it quickly. I don't want anyone to get the wrong impression about us."

Does she know how pretty her smile is? "Understood. We'll make it quick."

He led her to the small room he used as an office. He poured her a cup of java. She studied him. "You be okay, I mean really?"

"Why do you ask?"

"Your eyes, lately there's been something in them that I'm concerned about."

"What do you mean?"

She nibbled her cookie. "Do you like these?"

"They're really good."

That smile was back. "I was thinking of you while I made them."

Now Isaac felt his cheeks heat. "Getting back to my eyes..."

"You look hurt. I'm really concerned about you."

"I'm fine."

"What happened?"

He shivered as he thought about what had happened in the barn. "I, uh, it's nothing..."

He was surprised when she reached over and warmly touched his hand. He almost fell off the chair when she spoke. "Isaac, you are my closest friend and I care about you. If you don't want to talk, I understand, but know... I'm here for you." That was the first time she'd said his name that way.

"I really messed up."

She leaned back. "How?"

"I gave in to temptation and I, I led someone on. She's in a serious relationship."

Her face paled. "How did you tempt her?"

"I kissed her."

"And now how do you feel?"

"Horrible. Suppose that moment of stupidity comes between them and they break up or something? I couldn't live with myself."

Rebecca nodded, as if she understood. "Have you asked the Lord for forgiveness?"

"Yes, I did."

"Then He's forgiven you already. There's just one thing more to do."

Isaac couldn't miss the twinkle in her eye. "What's that?"

"Ask the Lord to help you to forgive yourself."

She's so wise. She might look young, but inside, she was filled with years of wisdom. "Good advice."

Rebecca stood. "Thank you for the coffee. I spoke with my father. He told me to invite you to Thanksgiving meal with us. We'd like you to learn more about our ways," her voice trailed off, "before..."

"Before?"

Her face turned pink. "We eat the meal at two. Will you come, English?"

A thought entered his mind. "Do *you* want me to?"

Her cheeks were now blood red. "Yes. That would please me very, very much."

"Okay. What should I bring?"

"Your appetite... and an open mind."

***

Kim held Rachel's chair while she sat down. The scent of fresh brewed tea filled the entire tea room. Since that night in the classroom, Kim had been taking it slow, but Rachel's feelings hadn't. They'd grown into something... *like love?*

"Thank you for bringing me here. I love this place."

"Yeah, me too."

She saw him stiffen and his face turned pale. Kim's eyes were focused behind her. Rachel turned. A woman with long strawberry-blonde hair walked forward until she stood before them. The lady held a small child. A pretty teenager stood by her side and had her arm around a cute little girl about Grey's age. The woman smiled. "It's nice to see you again, Kim."

"Good afternoon, Hannah." Rachel could tell he was shaken. "This is my friend, Rachel Domitar. Rachel, this is Hannah Espenshade and her daughters, Beth and Missi. And this is the first time I've actually met this little girl. Sorry, Rachel." Kim seemed to remember his manners. "Hannah married Sam, Jenna's brother."

That's why he's upset. Rachel extended her hand toward the other lady. "I'm pleased to meet you. Kim speaks fondly of your husband."

"Thank you. Jenna meant a lot to Sam." Hannah turned and faced Kim. "So much that he named our youngest daughter after her. Kim, Rachel, this is Jenna Lynn Espenshade."

Rachel turned at the sound of Kim's sob. The deep breath was ragged. "May I hold her?"

Hannah nodded and handed the little girl to him. Kim quickly brushed his cheeks. "She's so beautiful." He whispered to the little girl. "Hi, Jenna. I hope you realize you've got big shoes to fill. Your namesake was very special. You could say your aunt was perfect." His voice was louder when he addressed Hannah. "She's got her daddy's eyes. Let's hope she gets her looks from her mommy though."

After Hannah and her girls departed, Kim's eyes were distant. He jumped when Rachel spoke. "Jenna must have been a special woman."

"She was. Anyone who spent more than thirty seconds with Jenna knew she was exceptional. And she loved kids. We were planning on having three of our own, someday. Did I tell you Jenna was a kindergarten teacher?"

"No. It was nice of her brother to name the baby after her."

Kim's eyes seemed watery. "Jenna and Sam had a special bond. We joked about it a lot, but I always knew she loved her brother more than she could ever love me. He was a baseball star. Some of it was natural ability, but I believe most of the credit belongs to his sister. She sure did love her brother."

Rachel held his hand. "This has to be hard. If you don't want to talk about it, I understand."

It appeared he hadn't heard her. "I should have died alongside her during that trip. She asked me to go along, but I was selfish. I stayed here because of a school event."

"What happened?"

"Sam was in the playoffs. He led his team to the championship, and they won, because of him. Jenna

99

called me that night. She was so excited. Sam was going to the major leagues. She asked if I would mind if the two of them took off for a few days. Jenna told me their worlds were about to change. He was heading to the pros and we were getting married in the spring." Kim shook his head and met her gaze. "I never could tell her 'no'. Wish I knew then what I know now. I would have somehow dissuaded her from going."

"What happened?"

"They were driving back on the turnpike when a deer ran in front of them. Her car ended up at the bottom of a ravine. Sam and Jenna were missing for two days before the State Police found them. Jenna didn't make it."

"I'm so sorry."

"Sam was really messed up. His busted leg ruined his career, but his worst scars were the ones no one else could see."

"I guess seeing your sister die would mess anyone up."

"It was the way it happened. Jenna died in his arms. He was covered in her blood and couldn't get away from her body. For two days. Sam lost his mind."

"I don't know what to say."

Kim wiped his cheek again, yet he was smiling. "Do you know what finally brought Sam out of it and saved him?"

"No."

"That lady you just met, Hannah. She did. Sam told me about the last conversation he and Jenna had. She told Sam that God promised her He would send someone to replace Jenna as his best friend. And you just met her." Kim reached across the table, touched Rachel's chin and then turned her head so they were looking into each other's eyes. "Do you know what Jenna told Sam about me?"

An eerie feeling was crawling up her neck. "No."

"Jenna told him I would find the love of my life. For years, I fought letting her go. The hardest thing to ever happen in my life was losing her. I can't tell you how many hours I've spent in therapy. Earlier this year, I stopped by Jenna's grave to tell her I was moving on."

Rachel shivered. "Kim..."

"I felt her spirit. It was like she gave her approval."

Rachel had no clue how to respond. He didn't seem to notice. "And now, there's just one thing to ponder."

"What's that?"

The intensity of his eyes was almost magnetic. "Are you the one Jenna was talking about? Are you the love of my life?"

***

Joe threw another log on the fire. "Do you want to watch another movie?"

Leslie shrugged. "It's up to you."

"You know, you can't tell my family we binge watch the Hallmark channel."

She nodded, but didn't make eye contact. "Your secret's safe with me."

I give her an opening to tease and she doesn't take it? "So, who is he?"

Her face turned bright red. "What do you mean?"

"The last time you acted this way, your client in Hanover was giving you a hard time. Tell me his name. I may not have graduated from Annapolis, but I do know a few Navy Seals who are looking for weekend work."

Leslie's color was returning to normal, but he noted she swallowed hard before speaking. "It's not a client."

"Problems with your new car?"

"It's running great."

"Do you have a headache?"

"No."

He placed his wrist against her forehead. "No fever, but it's as plain as the nose on my face."

"What? Something's wrong with my nose?"

Joe laughed. "Nope. But I know what's wrong and why you're so distant."

Redness again creeped into her cheeks. "Wh-what do you think's wrong?"

"Man trouble."

Her eyes widened. *I'm on a roll today!* It was rare that he could fluster Leslie. Sharp as a tack, her wit usually got the best of *him*. "I'm not s-s-sure what you're referring to."

"Would you like me to lay it out for you?"

"I, uh, I don't know."

"Ms. Lapp, I believe you're concerned about the upcoming cruise and the sleeping arrangements. I think you're worried that you might not be able to control your feelings when you have me all to yourself for seven days. In short, I suppose you're concerned your virtue might be in jeopardy."

Okay, if her face turned any darker red, it might look black. "Joe, I've never... we've talked about this."

He kissed her cheek. "Yes, yes. You and your old-fashioned beliefs. Alas, you'll be safe with me. Our cabin has two beds."

"Good."

"Well, was I right?"

She seemed even more confused. "About what?"

"Come on, Leslie. You don't seem to be with it tonight. Are you thinking about work, or not spending Christmas with your family, or the hole in the ozone layer? Inquiring minds want to know."

"I'm sorry. I know I haven't been myself lately..."

It was the slightest hint, but there seemed to be a smile waiting to be coaxed out. "Not yourself? Who are you? I like role playing, you know? Who are you trying to be? Some hot Hollywood starlet or a pop star?"

"No. I'm just a little blue, that's all."

"Hmm. From what I saw earlier, I thought you were a little red."

"Red or blue? Are we discussing politics?"

Joe couldn't help but laugh. Despite not being on top of her game today, she turned him on in a way no other woman ever had. In Leslie, he'd finally met his equal—in brains, wittiness and humor. And that combination had made him fall in love with this brown-haired, blue-eyed beauty. "It seemed you blushed a lot earlier. Wait, you don't have another man on the side, do you?"

She stood and her face again turned red, but he was pretty sure it was from anger this time. "Joseph

Rohrer, I get the distinct feeling you're harassing me tonight. And why? I don't even know. Are you upset because of my old-fashioned ways or because maybe I don't feel like joking with you this evening?"

He'd never seen this side of her. "Whoa. Take it down a notch, killer. I'm just calling 'em as I see 'em. It just seems like you've got a problem or something."

The rage in her eyes was probably visible from thirty-thousand feet. "Now I've got a problem? How about you quit hounding me?" She glanced at the wall clock. "Oh, look at the time. I'm really tired." She yawned, but he could tell it was forced. "Maybe we should call it a night. Studies show that one of the leading causes of people having problems is a lack of sleep."

His mouth fell open when she walked to the door and grasped his coat. He didn't even have the chance to respond. "Here you are, Doctor Rohrer. It's time for you to say goodnight."

Joe walked to Leslie and reached for her hand. She yanked hers from him. "Leslie, sweetie, I'm sorry. You know how we pick on each other and, you know, I guess maybe I took it too far."

She nodded. "Maybe I did, too. Still, I am pretty tired, so let's call it a night. Shall we?"

What did I do? "Okay. I guess I know where I'm not wanted."

Her nostrils flared and her words were measured. "Quit putting words in my mouth."

"I wasn't, Leslie. You know what, I think I should probably go."

"I agree that would be the best option... for both of us."

He walked onto the porch and turned to face her. "Would you like a goodnight kiss?"

She hesitated. Her eyes searched his and he felt naked before her. She shook her head and pursed her lips. "Not tonight. Goodbye, Joe. We'll talk soon."

The door closed in his face. *We'll talk soon? What just happened?*

Chapter Eight

Isaac walked into the kitchen. Grey was drinking orange juice and salivating over some toy flyers.

Despite looking exhausted, Connor was feeding his son. Aubrey was standing by the stove, frying bacon. "Morning."

Aubrey eyed him strangely. "What time did you get in last night?"

"It was probably pushing twelve-thirty."

"Hot date?"

"No. I got called in to repair the heating system in one of the hot houses. It was thirty-four degrees when I got there. Couldn't lose a whole building of cucumbers and beans, you know?"

Connor's voice sounded as tired as he looked. "And here we thought you were doing something fun."

"That was fun. It was a first for me."

Aubrey also looked drained.

"How about I finish breakfast and you sit for a bit?"

"If you wouldn't mind. I was going to make scrambled eggs to go with it."

Grey chimed in. "I want poached eggs." The little girl was so cute.

"How many?" Isaac asked.

"Three." Connor cleared his throat and Grey picked up on the non-verbal communication. "Please?"

"You got it, sweetheart."

Aubrey had plopped in her chair and closed her eyes.

"So, I take it Cooper kept you two awake?"

Aubrey replied without opening her eyelids. "Yeah, he was fussy pretty much all night long. I'm surprised you didn't hear it."

"I sleep like a rock since I left the military. It's easier to get a good night's sleep here in the civilian world when there's no one trying to kill you." Isaac dropped a chunk of butter in the frying pan. "You both look wiped. Is there anything I can do to help out?"

Connor quickly chimed in. "Want to stop at the grocery store after work? Even though we're eating over at Leslie's, we've got a lot of stuff to get."

Grey interjected. "Momma and me make cranberry slaw for the Thanksgiving meal. She puts a special ingredient in. Bet you can't wait to taste it."

Isaac set the timer for the poached eggs, then poured the scrambled eggs in another pan. "You'll have to save me some."

Aubrey's eyes were now open. "Hey, if Leslie didn't already invite you, I am. The meal's at her place at three-thirty. We typically go to Longwood Gardens afterwards, but I'll probably stay home with Cooper. I don't want him in the night air."

Isaac concentrated on stirring the eggs. "What time do you go to the Gardens?"

"We usually go around six-thirty. They always do a great job decorating."

"Well, I have other arrangements for the meal, but, if you want, I could babysit Cooper while you go."

It was easy to see the question on Aubrey's face. "Other arrangements?"

Isaac scooped the bacon out of the pan, placing it on paper towels to absorb the grease. "Rebecca Stoltzfus's father invited me to share the Thanksgiving meal with them."

All eyes were now on him. Grey spoke first. "Rebecca, our neighbor? The girl who rides her bike everywhere and likes you?"

It was getting warm in the kitchen. "We're just friends."

There was a look on Aubrey's face he'd never seen before. "I've lived here almost three years and they've never invited me over. I mean, when you see them outside, the Stoltzfuses are cordial, but to invite you to a meal, especially Thanksgiving? That's extraordinary. What's going on?"

"Nothing. Rebecca and I are just friends. I thought it was a nice gesture."

"Well yes, of course it is, but Isaac... it's Thanksgiving. To us, that means family time, as in together. Leslie loves family events. She'll be unhappy."

Par for the course. *I'm one big disappointment.* Since his blunder, he made sure to avoid all contact with Leslie. He still did the tasks around her house as he'd promised, but just made sure the two of them didn't talk. "I'm sorry. Maybe next year? Or how about Christmas?"

"Leslie won't be here for Christmas. She and Joe are going on a cruise."

Connor did a double take. "She's what? From when to when?"

Aubrey stared at her husband. "I thought she would have talked to you about it by now. She'll be gone for almost three weeks." Connor was staring at Aubrey like she had three heads. "Look, after Leslie told me, she asked me not to tell you. She wanted to let you know in person."

Her husband shook his head. "We have spent every single Christmas together, for my entire life. And now Joe Rohrer comes along and—"

Aubrey cleared her throat. "Grey, tell your uncle how many crackers you want with your eggs."

"Six."

Aubrey whispered. "What do you say?"

"Please?"

Isaac smiled. "You got it, kiddo."

Connor was shaking his head. "Sounds like our family traditions are falling apart." He glanced at Aubrey. "Are *you* planning on being here for Christmas?"

She laughed. "Of course. I wouldn't miss spending any holiday with you, dear." She turned to face Isaac. "Maybe you can do both dinners, you know, eat with the neighbors, then celebrate with us."

"We'll see."

"Is there a reason you don't want to eat with us?"

So I don't have to face Leslie. "Not really. Rebecca told me her father wants to talk to me about the Amish traditions."

"This is so strange. I've never heard anything like this before. Is there something going on between the two of you that you should tell your little sister about?"

"Come on. Like I told you, we're just friends. I'm sorry I said yes and will miss eating with you guys."

"It's okay, I guess."

Isaac carried the food to the table. "Here, to make up for it, we can eat breakfast together."

Aubrey engaged his eyes. "Thanks for cooking, but that's not what I mean. I'm frustrated you won't be sharing Thanksgiving with us. You do realize you are family, don't you?"

She was always so kind. Not for the first time, he regretted not being close with her during their youth. "Yes. In word and deed, you've made me feel welcome."

"Good. I do ask one thing, though."

"What's that?"

She didn't answer right away. There was something new in her gaze. "*You* have to tell Leslie you're not coming. In person."

***

"I want you to meet my family. My mom told me to ask you to Thanksgiving."

The light in Kim's eyes was so bright these days. Maybe what Jenna told her brother was true. *Could I really be the love of his life?* She hoped so. "I, uh, told Leslie I'd be there for her meal."

He did that thing. The one where he pushed his lips to the side and looked up to his left. That meant he was thinking. It was so adorable. "What time is her meal?"

"I think three-thirty. What time does your family celebrate?"

A wide smile split his face. "This will be perfect. My mom serves the meal at noon, but our celebration begins with Thanksgiving breakfast and, of course, watching the Macy's Thanksgiving Day parade. Mom makes monkey bread and Bananas Foster."

"What? You eat monkey meat and drink alcohol for breakfast? Is that a Lancaster County thing?"

His laugh was contagious. "No, it's a cinnamon bread type of pastry... absolutely no meat in it whatsoever. And the refreshments are virgin. It's quite rare for my family to even have a glass of wine."

"What about Leslie's meal?"

"You can still make it. I'll drop you off back at her house."

"Will you stay?"

"For the meal?"

"Yes."

His eyes lit up. "I'm invited?"

"If Leslie doesn't invite you, then I won't be there. But I'm sure she won't mind." Rachel grew quiet for a moment. "The Lapps are my family now. My parents are gone and..." She couldn't continue.

Kim wrapped his strong arms around her. "It's okay. When times get tough, I'll be your anchor. When you're too weary to take one more step, I'll carry you. I hope you know this by now. I love you, Rachel."

Her eyes flew open wide. Despite the talk about wondering if she was the love of his life, he'd never said it. Her lips allowed the inner-most thoughts of her heart to escape. "I love you, too."

She pulled his face toward her and their lips met for the first time. And just like she'd dreamed, fireworks exploded in her head.

After the kiss, they rubbed noses. He finally returned to his seat. Rachel wiped her lips with a napkin. "Everyone's looking."

He laughed. "So? I don't care. It's not like we're in the school cafeteria."

"Yep, but none of the other people here at Shady Maple Smorgasbord are making out."

"Do you see a lot of kids here?"

"Yes."

"I bet their parents made out somewhere along the line."

"Kim Landis!"

"Sorry, I like letting my hair down when I'm with you. There are so many things I like about you."

"Hi, Mr. Landis."

Rachel turned her head. A well-built dark-haired beauty stood before them. Rachel saw how Kim's eyes popped. "Miss Lee. It's been quite a while. How have you been?" He slid over and motioned for the Asian lady to sit next to him. "I haven't seen you in what, eight years?"

"Something like that." She turned and nodded at Rachel. "Who's your friend?"

Kim's face flushed. "This is Rachel Domitar. Rachel, this is Aiko Lee. She student-taught under me a while back."

"Pleased to meet you, Rachel."

"Likewise. Aiko is a beautiful name. What does it mean?"

"Love child. There was a great difference in age between my parents. He was her teacher at university and well, I was the result of a passionate evening. It happens more frequently than one might expect."

Wow. Talk about TMI. "What do you teach?"

"Communications. I actually just moved back to Lancaster from the west coast." She trained her eyes on Kim. "Do you know of any openings?"

He couldn't seem to take his eyes off of Aiko. "Actually, you're just a tad late. We had an opening for a drama teacher and I hired Rachel."

"Ah, and you're out to dinner together. I should have guessed." She stood and smiled at Rachel. "It was a pleasure to have met you. Congratulations."

"For what?"

"Getting the drama position." Aiko winked at her. "Kim loves playing, I mean, plays. He likes drama, you know?"

To Rachel's total surprise, the girl swooped down and kissed Kim on the lips. "Nice to see you again. Maybe we can catch up sometime?"

He answered, "Maybe. We'll see." She walked off, swinging her hips to accentuate her extremely well-toned posterior. Kim gulped. "It's a long story."

Rachel pushed back from the table and made herself comfortable. "I'm listening."

***

Why did this have to happen now? Things had been progressing so well with Rachel. "Aiko student-taught for me a couple of years ago."

"The way she said goodbye leads me to believe the two of you had more than a professional relationship."

"We were close."

"Apparently so."

"She liked to flirt, but I ignored it, until..."

The glare from her eyes was like the beam of a spotlight. "Until? If you were serious about that 'love of your life' line from the other day, you'd better start communicating."

"You're right. After her last class, I took her out to dinner. She asked if I could come back to her apartment and help her box up a few things. She was moving back to college to finish her last semester." He had to stop.

Rachel looked so disappointed. "But let me guess, when you got there, not a lot of packing got done, did it?"

I'd give anything to be anywhere but here. "Nope. We ended up making out, pretty heavy duty."

"Were you engaged to Jenna at the time?"

"No. It was actually just before I met Jenna."

"Was it just the one time, or..."

"I drove out to her college to see her a couple of times after that. It didn't take long until we both realized it wasn't going to work, so we parted ways."

"And that was it?"

He drew an 'X' across his chest with his finger. "This evening was the first time I've seen her or spoken with her since then."

"I can't believe you slept with a student-teacher."

"Wait. We might have made out, but we didn't sleep together, ever. Believe it or not, I do have the slightest bit of morality running through my veins."

Rachel ran her hand through her hair. "That's encouraging, but answer this for me. Aiko asked about the job. When you told that girl you'd hired me, she said she wasn't surprised we were out to dinner together. Was she just talking about the relationship the two of you had or something else? What am I missing? Do you make it a point to date people that work for you?"

Kim could feel the heat grow in his cheeks. "No. I've only ever dated two women who worked under me. She was the first and you are the second. And asking you out had absolutely nothing to do with me being your boss. Instead, it was how you make me feel inside."

Rachel scrutinized him. "Before or after you hired me?"

"I don't understand. Why would that make a difference?"

"Did I get the job based on my merit and abilities or was it because you were attracted to me?"

"I made a professional decision when it came to the job. You're talented and great at what you do, and I'd hire you again. In a heartbeat. And if you need to know the truth, I told HR to make a job offer before we'd even met."

She shook her head and looked down at the table. "Well, one thing about tonight, it made me realize things have been going way too fast."

The bitterness of dread filled him. Her vision seemed focused on something that wasn't really there. *Is she thinking about the man who left her standing at the altar?* "I'm sorry."

Rachel sighed and looked away. "Yeah. Me, too."

***

Leslie heard the squeak of the front door as it opened. "Hey, sis? Are you in here?"

"I'm in the kitchen."

The entrance to the kitchen swung open and in walked her brother. Connor sure didn't look happy this morning. "Can we talk for a few moments?"

"I've got to get going shortly. Have an appointment down in Glen Rock, you know, in York County."

"I know my geography. I drive for a living, remember?"

"What's stuck in your craw this morning?"

He shifted his weight. "Until Aubrey came along, you were my closest friend. What happened?"

She sighed. *Not more conflict.* "I don't have time for an argument. What did I do now?"

He recoiled. "Now? First off, don't act like I'm a bother to you."

"You've been a bother since the day you were born."

"Let's step past the usual veil of insults. This is serious. Why didn't you tell me?"

"Tell you what?"

"About this cruise."

"Oh, that. Joe and I decided to take a little vacation, that's all."

Her brother's eyes narrowed. "Over Christmas?"

"There wasn't a lot of choice with the itinerary. Joe said this is a repositioning cruise."

"And you're fine with not being home over the holiday... your only nephew's *first* Christmas? Not to mention Grey. She's tottering on the edge of belief in Santa Claus. This might be the final year for her."

This is the last thing I need today. "Connor, don't do this."

"You and I have spent every single Christmas of my entire life together. Some of the greatest memories I've ever had were shared with you on Christmas Eve and Day. Until *he* comes along."

Leslie got in her brother's face. "Look. You have Aubrey. I've had no one, until now. And for the first time in my life, there's someone I want to share it with. A person who makes me happy. And what does Connor do? He wants to take it away from me, to control me. I certainly didn't expect this flak from you. I'm having a hard-enough time with... things."

Connor nodded, but the disappointment in her was plain to see. "And you're too blind to see it. Joe's forcing you to decide between your family and his."

"Grow up! He's not like that."

"Really? Who else is going along?"

A coldness fell on her shoulders. "J-just us. Why would you think there's anyone else going? You're just jealous I found a man. It spites you to see me happy, doesn't it?"

Her brother engaged her eyes. "Believe it or not, I love you and I wish you every blessing you could ever imagine. There's simply one thing that bothers me."

"Like what?"

"Maybe I'm wrong, but I seem to recall something Joe once told me."

"And that would be?"

"About the annual Rohrer family vacation. Since I've known Joe, his family has made it a tradition to take a trip together over the Christmas holiday."

"But we're not going with his family. It's just the two of us."

Connor shook his head and readied to leave. "Are you positively sure about that?"

"A hundred percent."

"Maybe you should verify that with him."

Chapter Nine

L eslie slipped the ham into the oven and programmed the timer. Soft cries from the next room brought a sad smile. Being around Connor and Aubrey's infant son had stirred something deep inside her soul.

"Want me to peel the potatoes?" Aubrey stood in the doorway, watching her.

"You don't have to. You can watch the parade with Connor if you'd like."

Aubrey giggled. "I think I'd rather help you. I'm beginning to miss adult conversations and besides, Connor really should have a little bonding time with his son."

Leslie shook her head. "My brother always did try to shirk his duties. Where'd Grey go this morning?"

"She and Isaac drove down to the Buck, to Mud Run. My brother said he saw a bald eagle there last week and he took Grey this morning to see if he could find it again."

Leslie opened the ten-pound bag and dumped the potatoes onto the table. She retrieved two peelers, a paring knife and the big colander. "Isaac stopped by the other night and told me he wouldn't make it today."

"Good. I told my brother that he needed to tell you in person."

"Well, he did. Isaac said he's eating with the Stoltzfuses today. I'm beginning to think there's something going on between him and that Rebecca girl."

"I don't know her that well. Is she the oldest of their children?"

"Yes. She's in Rumspringa."

Aubrey dropped the first peeled potato into the strainer. "What's that?"

"It's the coming of age for the Amish youth. Rebecca started it a little late, but basically the Amish youth get to try out the evils of our English world before they get baptized in their church. And I'm concerned about Isaac."

"Why?"

"I think Rebecca has designs on him. Even Grey told me she thinks Rebecca likes him."

"Keep in mind, Grey's only nine. Besides, Isaac tells me they're just friends."

Leslie scratched her nose with the back of her hand. "Don't you find it strange they invited him to dinner?"

"Isaac said Mr. Stoltzfus wanted to tell him about the Amish ways and customs."

Leslie dropped her potato peeler. "He said what?"

"Isaac said—"

"I heard you, but it just struck me as to why."

Aubrey reached for another potato. "Don't keep me in suspense. Spill the beans."

"I've heard that Rebecca's grandmother was an English girl, like us. That is until she met Amos Stoltzfus while he was on Rumspringa. They fell in love, but he wanted the plain life. To everyone's surprise, she was the one who converted. The girl learned the ways and customs of the Amish, got baptized in their church and married Amos. I'd bet my business that's what Rebecca has up her sleeve."

Aubrey tried not to let it, but laughter found its way out. "You and your imagination."

Leslie was finding it hard to breathe. "I don't think this is a laughing matter."

"Can you see him in a straw hat... and suspenders? Holding a little girl in a black dress and a son in a pastel shirt. How cute!"

Leslie's nose started tingling. She rubbed it hard to drive off the feeling. "I don't think this is the least bit funny. Your brother would miss all the modern conveniences, not to mention that pickup he loves. Devo looks so happy, handsome and proud when he's mowing our lawn. No, he shouldn't be with Rebecca. He can't."

Aubrey was watching her with profound interest. "Our lawn? Leslie, who should he be with?"

Me, but I can't tell you that. Her cheeks warmed. "I don't know... I'm just concerned about his happiness. He wouldn't enjoy the plain life. Can we change the subject?"

Aubrey's words were soft and slow. "If that's what you really want. But I want to say something first. If you ever want to talk about your feelings or anything else, I'm always here. I'm not just your sister-in-law, I'm your friend. And anything you say to me goes no further, and that includes Connor."

Leslie dropped her potato and grabbed Aubrey. "I'm so glad I convinced my brother to marry you."

Aubrey snickered. "Me, too. And isn't it amazing how things worked out?"

"What do you mean?"

"Well, when Joe came to the Labor Day party a couple of years ago and met you, none of us had any idea you'd just met your future boyfriend. Of course, we had that little blow up when I picked Connor over him. But when your car broke down last April, who came to your rescue? The tall, handsome Dr. Joseph Rohrer."

"Stop it. You'll make me blush."

"You always say everything happens for a reason."

"I do, don't I?" Leslie was quiet. *God, why did you bring Devo into my life?*

Aubrey peeled the next potato in silence. Her voice was soft. "Are you happy?"

"Of course. Why do you ask?"

"I can read you like a book, and I'm getting the feeling you just fibbed to me. Sure you don't want to talk about it?"

Leslie's hands were shaking. "Did you ever have second thoughts, about marrying Connor?"

"No."

"What about Joe? Ever wonder what it might have been like?"

"No. Connor and I were meant to be."

"Did you love Joe?"

Aubrey set down the utensil so she could give Leslie her full attention. "I did, but I also loved Connor."

"I'm glad you did, but why did you choose Connor over Joe? I mean, Joe's better looking... polite and kind... but you picked my runny-nosed kid brother instead of rock star Joe. Help me understand this."

Aubrey's eyes were brimming with kindness and understanding. "Yes, Joe is all those things. In a side-by-side comparison, it would be logical for any girl to pick Joe. But there was something about your brother. He's filled with compassion and acts on it, because it comes from his heart. Think back to when you fell off that cruise ship. Connor didn't hesitate risking his life when he jumped in to save you. And when that maniac attacked me on the train, Connor stepped in to protect me. He didn't even know who I was."

Aubrey's son started crying again. The sound of Connor's voice came through the door. "Aubrey? Honey? Can you come help me? I don't know what he needs."

"I'll be right there."

Leslie wiped her cheeks and giggled. "Yes, Connor may be all those things, but he's still rather helpless. Always has been."

Aubrey squeezed her hand. "Thankfully Connor had you to help him. To be on his side." Aubrey's eyes led her smile. "And just so you know, I'll always be on *your* side. If I can offer you any advice, it would be to have the courage to follow your heart. It worked for me." Aubrey hugged her and departed to help her husband.

Leslie bowed her head. "Lord, I'm not the smartest person right now. I'm confused. Please, show me the way."

The squeaking of the front door interrupted her prayer. Shivers rolled down her spine as she listened to the conversation and recognized the speaker. Devo had stopped by to drop off Grey. A voice seemed to whisper in her ear. *Here's your answer, child.*

***

Kim held the door for Rachel as she climbed into the very rear seat of Leslie's SUV. Kim plopped down next to her. In the middle row sat Aubrey and Grey and Connor. Devo stayed back to babysit Cooper and allow Connor and Aubrey time with Grey. Joe Rohrer dropped into the shotgun seat after assisting Leslie. They were headed to Longwood Gardens to view the Christmas lights. Another Lapp tradition they shared with Rachel. *Our family traditions.*

Kim's whisper caught her attention. "Thank you for a wonderful day. In case you didn't know it, my parents loved you."

After the sudden appearance of Aiko, Rachel had decided she and Kim needed to slow things down. But there was a problem with that. A big one. Her heart didn't agree with the decision and continued to pull Kim Landis deeper into her soul. "I had a really nice time as well."

His fingers touched her chin and turned her head until they were eye to eye. "And thank you for inviting me to share the meal with your family. I'm stuffed, but I'm hoping we'll get used to this."

"Used to what? Eating too much?"

"No, silly. Visiting both of our families on holidays. And who knows? Maybe one day we'll be the ones hosting Thanksgiving."

Their lips hadn't met since that woman interrupted their meal, but Rachel was losing the battle to resist him. When he leaned close, Rachel moved to meet his lips.

"Momma, look. Aunt Rach is kissing Mister Kim. Yuck!"

Rachel's entire body tensed and she pulled away at Grey's words.

Aubrey shook her head. "Greiston, that was rude not only to watch what they were doing, but to tell everyone what's happening back there. Please apologize to Rachel and Kim."

In the passing illumination of headlights, Rachel could see Grey turn to her. "Sorry, Aunt Rach, Mister Kim."

Rachel tousled the little girl's hair. "That's okay."

Connor entered the conversation. Of course, his voice had that tone. The teasing quality. "Now Grey, when two people love each other, they kiss a lot. I mean, you see me kiss Momma a lot."

Leslie joined in the teasing. "Oh gross. Poor Aubrey. Are your vaccinations up to date?"

Connor continued. "And I'm sure you've seen Joe kiss your Aunt Leslie." He paused briefly. "Brave man that he is. So, I believe it's only natural for Aunt Rachel and Mister Kim to kiss."

"But you and Momma are married, so you can kiss. They're not."

Rachel's eyes widened when she heard Kim mutter, "Yet."

Aubrey advised her daughter, "You're too young to understand. Why, I bet someday you'll meet a prince and fall in love. And you'll want to kiss him."

Connor piped up. "But not until you're forty-five, at least."

The little girl was inquisitive. "Does it feel good when you and Momma kiss?"

"Of course."

"How about you, Aunt Leslie? Does it feel good when you and Joe kiss?"

Leslie acted quickly to change the subject. "Grey, look. We're in Chatham."

"So?"

"There's a very mysterious place here in Chatham."

"Yeah?"

Connor laughed. "She's talking about the CIA spy house."

CIA spy house? Rachel broke into the conversation. "I don't think I've heard about this."

Aubrey laughed. "It's a story the two Lapp siblings made up. You see, there's this really tiny diner down here."

Connor added, "The building is maybe thirty square feet."

Rachel had to giggle when she saw the look Aubrey gave her husband. "Thank you, sweetheart, for interrupting. Anyway, the diner has a sign stating it's only open from five until nine in the morning, weekdays only."

Leslie interrupted. "Which would make one believe they offer breakfast, but—"

Connor finished, "We've never seen a car there, like ever."

"So why do you think it's a spy house?" Kim asked.

"It's too small to be a diner," Leslie said. "Never any cars there, but they're still in business. I believe there's this giant complex underground and that building is where the spies enter the control center."

Joe groaned from the front seat. "You're crazy. I've eaten there many times and the food is tops."

Leslie admonished him. "That explains a lot."

"Yeah, thanks for bursting my bubble," Connor said. "Next, you'll tell me Neil Armstrong really didn't walk on the moon."

The adults all laughed.

"So, are you two all prepared for your cruise?" Kim asked. "Have you picked out excursions yet?"

The cabin was suddenly quiet, until Grey said, "What's an extursion?"

Aubrey explained, "Excursion, honey. It's when the ship stops in a port, people get off and do things to see the area."

Kim added, "When I was younger, my parents took me on a cruise to the Caribbean. On one island, we got to swim with the dolphins."

Joe laughed. "We did that one, too. My sister Frannie loves dolphins. I know she wants to do it on this cruise, but Leslie and I haven't talked about it yet."

The big Chevy swerved for a second. Leslie's voice seemed tinged with anger. "On this cruise? Is your sister going along? I thought you said it was the two of us, alone."

"Of course it's the two of us, in our stateroom. This is one of our traditions. My family always takes a trip over the holiday."

"Didn't I tell you?" Connor said.

Aubrey reached over Grey and pinched her husband at the same moment Leslie yelled, "Shut up, Connor! Now's not the time."

Rachel could feel the tension in the vehicle when Joe responded. "What's the big deal? We do some of your family traditions, like tonight. Why can't we observe some of mine?"

The vehicle swerved again as Leslie directed her ire at Joe. "But you didn't even tell me your family was going along."

"And if I did, would you have said yes? It's not like I lied to you. I thought it would be best if I broke it to you slowly... over time."

"No, you didn't lie, but that's not the point. The point is you omitted things just to get your way." Leslie's voice was growing in volume. "That's known as manipulation and let me tell you something, Joseph, I will not allow *anyone* to control my life."

Rachel squeezed Kim's hand. The SUV kept drifting into the oncoming lane. She whispered, "I'm getting scared."

Aubrey must have heard her. "Leslie, with all due respect, maybe you should pull over. No offense, but you're all over the road and we have a child in the car."

Leslie all but screamed, "You know what, Aubrey..." All of the adults seemed to be bracing for an explosion. Leslie took a deep breath. "You are absolutely correct. I have a duty to protect the ones I love." She raised the turn signal and pointed the vehicle into an empty parking lot. "Mr. Rohrer, would you kindly step outside with me?"

Leslie slammed the door on her way out. The couple walked out of the beam of the headlights, but there was enough ambient light for everyone to observe the argument.

"I don't think I've ever seen Leslie this angry," Connor said.

Aubrey shook her head. "What Joe did wasn't right. And you getting in your jab certainly did not help the situation."

"I'm sorry."

"Remember to apologize to Leslie later."

Outside, Leslie turned from Joe. It was plain to see she was weeping. The doctor's body language clearly demonstrated his anger as he stormed to the vehicle and ripped the door open. "I'll say goodnight now and wish all of you a happy holiday season." His eyes glared at Connor. "And thanks, buddy. Thanks for stabbing me in the back a second time." He slammed the door shut so hard the entire vehicle shook, and then he headed off into the night.

Aubrey spoke quickly. "Connor, you drive. Grey, honey, can you shift up to the shotgun seat?"

"Why, Momma?"

"I think Aunt Leslie and I need some together time. We'll ride back here."

Poor Leslie. "Maybe Kim and I should move to the middle row so the two of you have more privacy."

"That might make her feel better. Thanks."

Everyone moved to their new positions. Aubrey and Leslie stood outside. Rachel remembered the promise they made to each other years ago. *Sisters until the end.* Before she could say anything, Kim whispered in her ear, "Go."

Rachel walked over to them. Aubrey handed Leslie a tissue.

Leslie's voice was weepy. "Guess I ruined tonight for everyone."

Rachel hugged her. "Shh. It will be fine, you'll see."

"This, this is the first time I've ever... ever broken up with a man. And I did it in front of my family. But the worst thing was I jeopardized everyone's safety. I'm so sorry. None of you will ever want to ride with me again."

Aubrey gently pushed the hair from Leslie's eyes. "Stop it. Of course we will."

"I never knew anything could hurt this bad. Even though he was the one in the wrong..."

Rachel squeezed her friend's hands. "I've been there and yes, it does hurt. But speaking from one woman to another, you will survive this. You'll come out happier than ever."

Leslie brushed her cheek. "When did you become a philosopher?"

Rachel's vision blurred as she remembered the pain. "I'm just repeating the words you told me. Remember? The words you said to me the night Eli left me standing at the altar."

Aubrey's voice was soft. "God has something special planned for you. Those were the words you told me when I first met you. Let that sink in and give you hope."

"Since when did you two ever listen to me?"

All three of them laughed. Rachel hugged her again. "We always do. Know why?"

"No. Tell me."

"Because you never stop talking."

Leslie smiled. Well, a little. "Figures. I need a friend and God sends you two."

Aubrey laughed. "We're better than friends."

"Yeah? Why?"

"Because we're sisters. Forever."

***

Isaac opened the door to the big work truck for Rebecca. It was late and they were on the way back from Green Dragon Farmer's Market. Neither of them usually worked the farmer's markets, but with the holidays and family gatherings, the two of them had drawn the assignment today.

She spoke after he climbed in. "I could get used to this, English."

She was funny, this Amish girl. In her speech and peculiar ways. He was glad they'd spent the day together. "Get used to what?"

The tone of her voice was softer now. "Spending time with you. Thank you for sharing Thanksgiving with my family. What did you think of the talk with my father yesterday?"

That was interesting. "I really enjoyed learning about the customs of your people. There are advantages to the simpler way of life."

"Aye, there are. Did he mention to you about my grandmother?"

"Yes. He remarked how she converted from Presbyterian into your faith."

Isaac pointed the truck left from State Street onto Route 322 East. Her tone was now inquisitive. "Is that something you would do?"

"Become Amish? I don't think I'd fit in very well in your faith. Besides, I've done lots of things that go against the kind, loving principles of your people."

He could sense her eyes on him. "Such as?"

"I was a United States Marine. I defended and fought for my country."

"Did you take life?"

Isaac drew a deep breath. "That's not a conversation you and I will ever have."

"Why not, Isaac?"

He noted she'd called him by his first name quite a few times today.

"Because I don't want you to think less of me."

The warmth of her hand against his arm startled him. He was even more surprised when she didn't move it away. "I've never thought more of any man than you. You could easily ask for forgiveness and repent. The Lord will grant it." She hesitated briefly. "I think you'd make a fine farmer... and, and a wonderful gut husband."

It was a good thing they were sitting at a stop light, because he might have run off the road. "Did I hear you right?"

There was enough light that he could see her face. Her eyes were glistening and her smile had never been as becoming as it now was. "Yes. I said a husband. As in... my husband."

Isaac's arms trembled as he gripped the wheel. The vehicle behind them blew their horn. Isaac saw the light was now green. He slowly accelerated. "Rebecca, how old are you?"

"Eighteen last March."

"I'm thirty."

She squeezed his arm. "Aye. I know that."

"That's twelve years difference in age—"

She quickly interrupted and it occurred to him she'd already considered his argument before he expressed it. "And it's just a number. Did you take notice to the man tending stand next to us, you know, for Hannah's Bakery?"

A mental picture of the young man who used a cane to get around formed in front of him. "Yes. Why?"

"That's Sam Espenshade. I know for a fact his wife is over twelve years older than him. And they are very happy together." She touched his cheek. "That, that could be you and me, Isaac."

"Rebecca, I don't mean to insult you, but I'd never make a good farmer and I'd be even worse at trying to be Amish. Wait. Is that why your father invited me to the Thanksgiving meal? Because you want me to become plain?"

"It was my grandmother's idea. She also thinks we'd be a good match for each other."

"Oh, Rebecca..."

"So you won't join the church?"

"I'm not going to lie to you. I won't ever do that."

They rode in silence until they were sitting at a stop light in Blue Ball. Rebecca broke the silence. "Well, I've thought this through. My grandmother told me I might have to do this."

He turned to her. To his utter surprise, she grabbed the back of his head and pressed her lips to his. She sighed as she pulled back. "Wow. Even better than I dreamed."

Isaac was shaking his head. "Stop. We can't do this again. This is wrong."

"Isaac, I want to do it, for you."

"No, no. You're a young girl and, and, this is absolutely not going to happen."

She grabbed his hand. "I've made up my mind. I'll leave the church, so you and I can be together."

"You'll what?"

"I'll turn my back on my community. You're a good man, Isaac. I can see us spending our lives together. I'll make you happy. I'll be a gut wife."

We need to talk about this. Isaac turned into an empty lot, set the brake and then turned to her. "Just slow down for a second. Did you listen to yourself?"

"Of course, I did. This isn't idle talk. I've thought of you every day since that first time I saw you at work. My affection for you has grown deeper since. This is what I want."

"But if you left the faith, you'd be shunned."

"By many in the community, yes."

"What about your family?"

She looked away. "That will be hard, but my grandmother told me they will come around in time. It's not as bad as it was in previous generations. In the old days, shunning meant you were dead to your family. Today, I would be an outsider, but can still visit wid them."

"But still…"

"Isaac, answer me this question. Do you not care for me? I feel that you do."

"Yes, I do care for you, but not in the way you think. This came as a total shocker. I, we… it just can't be."

Her eyes studied him. In them, he saw intelligence, wonder and, now that she brought it up, he saw love. "Before you say no, I want you to do this thing for me."

"What?"

"I want you to kiss me, as if we would be together forever. If you can do that, and your answer is still no," she sighed heavily, "we'll forget about tonight and mention this subject never again. Yes?"

He slowly nodded. Rebecca slid across the seat and held him tightly. He embraced her. She rubbed her nose against his and then softly kissed him. The warmth of her body and the pleasant taste of her lips was unexpected. In his mind, he could see them sharing life, holding hands as he introduced her to the wonders of his world. They separated for a second before she kissed him again, but with much more passion this time. The vision he'd had vanished when she sat back in the seat, wiping her mouth.

He didn't know why he was breathing so hard. "Rebecca?"

She studied him intently for a long moment before looking away. "Don't say it, Isaac. I can see in your eyes I'm not the girl you want." She slipped across the truck and stared out the window. "Can we head back to work now? It's late and I don't want anyone to get the wrong impression."

Chapter Ten

A ubrey placed the kettle of oatmeal on the table. She glanced over at Connor, who was feeding their son. Cooper didn't seem to be satisfied with just milk anymore, so they'd decided to try baby cereal. "Looks like somebody's enjoying his first taste of cereal."

Grey had a big smile on her face. "Can I feed him, please?"

Grey was such a pleasant and loving child. It was a shame her own parents didn't want her. *Thank You for letting us adopt her.* "As soon as you finish eating, I think that would be fine."

A shuffling noise distracted Aubrey. Isaac had found his way into the kitchen. He looked exceptionally haggard this morning. Her brother nodded. "Good morning, everyone."

"I made oatmeal for breakfast, with apples, walnuts and brown sugar. You hungry?"

"Maybe a little. I'll make coffee. Anyone else want some?"

There was something about his expression that bothered Aubrey. "Maybe one cup."

Grey chimed in. "I'd like one."

Aubrey shook her head. "It will stunt your growth."

Connor chuckled. "Maybe we should start her on java. I'd like to keep her like this forever."

Grey's lips curled in disgust. "Na-uh. I'm growing up. I want to be a business woman, like Momma."

Isaac handed a steaming cup to Aubrey. "Here you go, sis."

"Didn't see you yesterday. Everything go well at work?"

He swallowed hard. "Let's just say the day's past and that's a good thing."

"How was your Thanksgiving with the Stoltzfuses?"

"They were pleasant." She noted how quickly he changed the subject. "How was your evening at Leslie's?"

"Aunt Leslie and Joe had a big fight," Grey said. "They broke up."

Aubrey watched her brother's reaction. His eyes grew as big as dinner plates and his face lost all color.

"Grey, honey, that's an adult thing," Connor said. "It's not your place to tell people about Aunt Leslie's business."

The admonition didn't seem to affect the little girl. "Sorry."

The concern in Isaac's eyes was fascinating. "Is she okay?"

"No, she's having a rough time."

Isaac shook his head. "He's an idiot. Leslie's a wonderful lady."

Aubrey caught the look Connor shot at him. "Leslie? A lady? I think you've been sniffing too many diesel fumes."

Isaac stood and faced Connor. "Excuse me for saying this in your house, but you ought to try being a little nicer to your sister. The way you always insult her isn't becoming. It's downright offensive to me."

Now Connor gave Aubrey a puzzled look before turning to her brother. "Sorry, Isaac. Let me explain something. Leslie and I love to tease each other. And we often hurl insults at one another, as a funny thing. Neither of us mean anything by it. I love my sister as well as respect her. After Aubrey, Leslie is my closest friend and always will be. Thought you picked up on that fact by now, but I wanted to spell it out in case you didn't."

Her brother nodded and sat down. "Sorry, Connor. I over-reacted."

Aubrey could still feel tension. "What are you doing today?"

"I dunno."

"We're going to get our Christmas trees. Our family tradition is that we go pick out a tree together and cut it down. Later this afternoon, we'll decorate, both here and at Leslie's. You know, part of this tradition is stopping at Miller's Smorgasbord for lunch first. Why don't you join us?"

"Maybe. I've got an errand to run first."

"Yeah? What are you doing?"

He carried his empty bowl to the sink, rinsed it out, then placed it in the dishwasher. "What am I doing? Something I should have done weeks ago."

***

Isaac pulled his old pickup into the drive of the two-story colonial situated next to the golf course. The one belonging to the country club. It surprised him that he'd been able to reach Rachel on her cell and it amazed him even more that she knew where the good doctor lived. He had to dance a little and tell a white lie that he owed Joe some money and needed to repay the man.

Hope he's home. Isaac only had so much courage, but he needed to do this thing. As soon as Grey had blurted it out that Leslie and Joe had broken up, Isaac knew he was to blame. The things he'd done in the service of his country that had earned him medals took less bravery than this mission would. What was he supposed to tell Joe? *I, uh, tempted your girl until she kissed me and, um, that's why you had your argument.* Yeah, right. He expected Rohrer would punch him. And he deserved it. Isaac was no better than the men who had seduced his ex-girlfriend.

Nevertheless, Isaac dismounted and trudged the seemingly miles long, brick walkway to the porch. It took all of his mettle to ring the doorbell. Within seconds, the polished mahogany door opened. Joe Rohrer stared back at him with angry eyes.

"Morning, Dr. Rohrer."

"What's good about it? What can I help you with, Mr. Golden?"

This is gonna be harder than I thought. "I understand you and Leslie broke up."

The man was seething. "And what business is it of yours? Did Leslie send you?"

"No, sir. I came of my own volition. I actually came to apologize and confess."

"Confess what?"

Isaac tried to swallow, but had trouble getting the lump to stay down. "Sir, I know I'm the reason the two of you broke up. I'd like to explain and beg you to forgive Leslie."

The doctor shook his head. "This ought to be good. What do you think you possibly did that had any bearing whatsoever on our split?"

"Sir, it was my fault. I overstepped my boundaries and I, uh, I tempted her. I kept it up until she kissed me. And for this, I'd truly like to—"

"Excuse me? She did what?"

"Kissed me, sir."

"When did this gem of an event occur?"

"Just before Halloween."

"Let me see if I've got this straight. You came here to tell me this so you could have a clear conscience?"

"No, sir. I came to your home in hopes you could forgive her and the two of you could be whole again."

Rohrer started laughing. "I'm such an idiot."

Not what I expected, but we can work with that. "Come again?"

"Golden, you're looking at a fool. I sure know how to pick them."

"What do you mean, sir?"

"First, your two-timing, faithless, double-crossing sister picked that loser she married over me. Then Leslie turns out to be a world-class tramp. Whether or not you tempted her, the little harlot should have controlled herself. But instead, she let some dumb redneck pick her up. Are you sure you only kissed her, nothing more?"

Isaac could feel his anger spiraling out of control. "Let's get something straight. I could care less what you say about me, but I will not tolerate you calling either Aubrey or Leslie names. Take it back... *now*."

Rohrer laughed. "Oh, I offended you? Here, let me tell you what I really think of those two little..."

As soon as the words left Rohrer's mouth, Isaac had no choice. He loved his sister and respected Leslie way too much to allow anyone to call them names, especially that word. He slugged Rohrer in the mouth and watched the good doctor crumple.

Rohrer held his hand to his bloody mouth.

It took all of Isaac's resolve not to finish the job. "Sorry, doc, but if I ever hear you call either of those ladies that word again, expect more of the same. Good day."

***

Rachel stirred her tea. Her mind drifted between two scenes—one occurring last night and the other on an evening nine years ago. "I really felt bad for Leslie last night."

Kim was sitting across from her. "I know. Joe was wrong. He should have been honest with her from the start."

Witnessing the breakup first-hand revived the bitter memory of how Eli had left, and the wound seemed as raw and painful as the day it occurred. "Yeah. People who try to hide things rarely get away with it. I can't believe he thought so little of Leslie."

They sipped their tea in silence. "I'm not one hundred percent sure you're talking about Leslie exclusively. Just to make it clear, I wasn't trying to hide what happened with Aiko from you."

Felt like you were. "That was quite a surprise, not only hearing about what happened from her, but just the fact that she showed up in the first place." Rachel shook her head. "You've got to give it to Aiko, she certainly knows how to make an entrance."

"Rachel, I made a mistake when I was younger. There's no way I can go back and change what happened. Can I ask why you're so upset?"

Rachel closed her eyes and took in the tangy scent of her lemongrass tea. "I'm sorry for making such a big deal out of this. It's just..." She allowed her voice to trail off.

Kim's fingers gently rubbed the skin on the back of her hand. "I don't want anything between us. Please talk to me."

The hurt of that far-off day once again filled her memory. "I had no clue he was in trouble. He hid it from me."

"Who?"

"It was supposed to be the happiest day of my life."

"Are you talking about your ex-fiancé?"

The server approached. "I'm sorry we're running behind this morning. One of our staff had car trouble and was late getting here. I just checked and your food should be coming up next."

Kim thanked the woman, then turned his attention back to Rachel. "Did you ever hear from him again?"

"No. He vanished and it was as if he'd never existed. For years, I believed one day I'd look up and he'd be there, but..."

"I can't fathom how difficult it must have been. And that's why it's so hard for you to trust?"

Her breath was ragged. "Not being able to trust has ruined every relationship I've ever had. Just when things begin to feel good, I start to worry and then I panic. I don't want to risk another heartbreak, so I run away."

Kim again touched her hand. "The last thing I want is for you to do that. We'll have to find a way for you to learn to trust... me."

"Sorry, Kim. I'm not an easy person to live with. You should probably just save yourself the trouble and forget about us. I'll end up hurting you. That seems to be my M.O."

Rachel concentrated on the floral design of her cup. The soft voice almost startled her. "I'll take my chances. I have an idea. Let's take the rest of the day and treat ourselves to a long drive together."

"To where?"

"I don't care. It's not about the destination, it's about spending time with you."

"I'd appreciate that, but we can't. I promised Leslie I'd help decorate this afternoon."

He did that thing again with his face when he was thinking. She couldn't help but smile. He held up his finger. "Maybe... I could tag along and be of assistance, too. And then, since we'd be in the Christmas spirit, perhaps we could make it a two-day event and decorate my tree tomorrow."

"Thought you wanted to take a long drive?"

"I'm flexible. And I hope you realize, I love spending time with you."

"Why?"

He reached across and touched her face. "Because I love you."

A chill rolled over her. "That's what Eli used to tell me, and we both know it didn't last."

Kim didn't reply immediately, but waited for Rachel to look up. "I'm not him. You know, words fade away, but actions speak louder than words. Let my deeds whisper to your heart and show you what forever can be."

***

Isaac lifted the turn signal and pointed the pickup toward Aubrey's house. Hopefully he'd arrive before everyone departed for the restaurant. His knuckles on his right hand throbbed. Glancing down, he saw the trickle of blood coming from the damaged skin of his middle finger.

In the distance, he caught sight of a bicycle coming toward him. His mouth was dry. *Rebecca.* She'd been on his mind since he dropped her off at the farm. He was very attracted to her, but it would never work. She was too young. And Isaac wasn't interested in joining her religion, or allowing her to turn her back on her family. But he'd hurt Rebecca. He was certain she didn't understand.

He slowed his truck to a crawl as she approached. Isaac wound the window down. "Morning, Rebecca."

Her eyes were focused straight ahead and didn't waver. Her reply was curt. "Morning, English."

That went well. He continued down the road until he reached Aubrey's house. Her minivan was missing. *Great. Strike two.* Isaac pulled out his cell and called his sister.

"Isaac. Where have you been? I was really hoping you were going to come along today."

"I am coming. I just got delayed, that's all. Am I too late?"

"No. We only left five minutes ago." Aubrey waited for a moment before continuing. "You said you had to run an errand. Where'd you go?"

"Oh, no place important."

"I see. Can I ask what you did?"

You might not understand, sis. "I was trying to right a wrong."

"Hmm. Did it have something to do with Joe Rohrer? Did you repay your debt?"

"How'd you know about that?"

"A little birdie told me."

Rachel. Isaac swallowed hard. "Maybe. Why?"

"Leslie received this cryptic text from Joe a couple of minutes ago."

"Really? What did it say?"

"I'll put Leslie on so she can read it to you."

"Uh, no, that's okay."

Leslie's voice came on. "Devo?"

"Oh, hi."

"Hi. I'm having a little trouble understanding this text. Can you help me?"

"I'll, I'll try."

"Good. It says, 'Next time your redneck lover boy comes over and punches me for no reason, I'll press charges.' You know anything about this?"

Great. Strike three. "Yep."

Chapter Eleven

L eslie scratched her head. *Where do we begin?*
"Connor, can you grab the decorations?"

"Of course, I can." Then he stood there, staring at her.

"They're up in the attic. Is something the matter?"

He had that goofy grin on his face. "Oh, you want me to go get them? I misunderstood, because you asked me if I was *able* to, not if I *would*. Guess they teach differently at a university than at a college." He turned to Devo. "You see, I went to Millersville University while my sister only went to a college. Alvernia College. There was a big difference in our education."

Leslie shook her head. "That's right. I went to a college where we studied actual subjects. What was that one course you had, 'Concepts in Math'? You remember, the course where you concentrated on one number each week and your assignment was to think about that number? Kind of reminds me of the 'think' method Professor Harold Hill used in *The Music Man*."

She was laughing inside and she knew that was Connor's goal—to take her mind off of the breakup. Leslie could tell by his expression that her brother was thinking of a snarky response. His eyes lit up. "It must have impressed my boss. You realize she hired me because of my brains. I am an engineer, after all."

"I'm still trying to figure out where you park your train."

Aubrey cleared her throat. "All of us enjoy the stand-up comedy, but there's a lot of decorating to do today." She turned to her brother. "Would you mind going up to the attic and start bringing down the boxes marked 'Christmas'?"

Isaac smiled. "Sure. How do I get there?"

Leslie noted the stink-eye look Connor shot his wife. "Come on, Isaac. Kim, you might as well come along. There's a lot of containers up there. We should probably call a company of stevedores to help us."

Aubrey balanced Cooper on one hip and placed her hand on the other. "Connor Lapp!"

"Going, dear."

Leslie had to hand it to her sister-in-law. She definitely knew how to keep Leslie's little brother motivated.

Grey yanked at Leslie's arm. "This is boring."

"Then let's make it fun. Let's ask Aunt Rach to put on some water for hot chocolate and in the meantime, why don't you find some music to put us in the spirit of the season?"

Without moving, Grey yelled, "Alexa, play holiday favorites."

"Wow. I'm pretty sure people in Philadelphia heard that one. Maybe you could go help Aunt Rach *find* the hot chocolate."

"Okay." The bundle of energy ran into the kitchen.

Thank You for a full house today, to keep my mind off of Joe. She almost jumped at the touch on her arm. Aubrey's eyes were watching her. "How are you holding up?"

"I'm surviving."

"Did you think about my offer?"

"Yes, but why would I sleep over at your house when mine is just a five-minute walk away?"

"Because Grey asked you to. We'll stay up late and watch movies. Eat popcorn. An old-time slumber party for us girls."

"Won't that keep the baby up?"

The smirk gracing her sister-in-law's face made Leslie laugh. "Connor wanted a son. Let him stand up to the plate and take a turn. Momma deserves a night off."

Leslie's smile faded as she thought of the other man who lived there. "It might keep Devo awake."

"I doubt that. He told me that one of the things the Corps taught him was how to fall asleep when ordered. I do believe my brother can sleep anywhere and anytime, on demand."

"I still can't believe he punched Joe. I'd have given anything to see that. I know what Devo told us, but why do you think he really went over?"

When Aubrey looked up and to the left, Leslie knew she was searching for something creative to say. In other words, to lie about it. *Why?*

"He's a simple and direct man. And like he says," Aubrey changed her tone to try and mimic the deeper voice of her brother. "Always faithful. To God, family and the United States Marine Corps, in that order. Semper Fi and oo-rah!"

"Oo-rah!" Both of them turned to find Isaac standing at the bottom of the stairs, holding a large Tupperware box with the words "C-mas decorations" written in Sharpie. "If I didn't know better, I'd think you two were making fun of me."

Leslie suspected someone in Heaven must have thrown a bucket of boiling water down on her, because her entire body was hot. "No, no. We were just talking."

"'Bout what?"

Cooper started to fuss. Aubrey used her son's cry as an excuse to jump ship. "I think I need to change somebody's diaper. We'll be back... later."

Devo shook his head and laughed. "That was obvious." He directed his attention back to Leslie. "I'm really sorry... about what I did to your boyfriend."

"Ex-boyfriend. Why did you go over there?"

"I know what I said earlier, but I owe you an honest answer." He sat the box down and moved until he was close enough to touch. "I went over there to confess."

The heat was now replaced by a chill. "Confess? What do you mean?"

"How I flirted with you when we were decorating the barn... and I kept it up until you kissed me..."

"Wait, you told Joe we kissed?"

"Yep. I also told him it was all my fault, but he didn't listen."

Her mouth seemed to be awfully dry. She rubbed her fingers at the corner of her lips. "How did he react?"

The man's eyes narrowed and she could touch his anger, if she would only reach her hand out. "He called both you and Aubrey a name that no civilized man *ever* uses to describe a lady."

"What word did he say?"

"Uh-uh, ma'am. I won't repeat it. I lost my temper and that's when I nailed him."

That makes more sense. "I still don't comprehend why you went to see him. And why did you tell him we kissed?"

He took such a deep breath that it seemed all the air in the room disappeared. Being this close and looking into his eyes, she suddenly felt faint.

"I know it's my fault the two of you broke up. I was trying to make it right by letting him know I was the one who tempted you. Your split was my fault and I was hoping my confession might make you two whole again."

Somehow, her hand moved to his cheek, as if he were magnetic and she were steel. "That was sweet, but the reason I broke up with him was because he lied. Well, not really lied. Let's just say he wasn't being entirely truthful with me. When I confronted him about it, he had a lot to say about how much he despised my family. He made it plain how the future would be. I couldn't tolerate it. My family means too much to me. That's why we broke up."

"I, I didn't know."

She brushed the hair from his eyes. "Guess we're a lot alike... in the devotion to our families, Devo."

He nodded. "I believe we are." The closeness between them shrank. Leslie's hand was now behind his head, ready to pull him in, like that night.

The laughing voice stopped the growing fantasy, "I see how it goes. Kim and I are left lugging all the heavy boxes while you two are goofing off. What are you doing, anyway? It looks pretty intimate over there." Connor and his smart attitude had returned.

Devo's cheeks were covered in red. Leslie answered for both of them. "Devo had a piece of glitter in his eye and I was getting it out."

"Sure you did. I wasn't aware that the Marines used glitter." Connor walked until he was standing right next to them. "Something new the Corps is trying out? And was it camouflage glitter?"

The grin on Devo's face couldn't be missed. "You're right. We tried, but it didn't work. Instead, we decided to stick with the old tried and true thing we do best."

Connor now stood next to them. "And that would be?"

He pivoted and faced Leslie's brother. "Punching annoying little brothers in the mouth." The ex-Marine shifted as if he was going to slug Connor.

Connor's eyes widened and he ran into the kitchen yelling, "Aubrey! Help!"

The man standing in front of her winked. "How'd I do?"

Leslie laughed. "Oo-rah."

***

156

As the afternoon progressed, Aubrey kept a close watch on both of the other couples. Kim was bending over backwards trying to cater to Rachel, but the emptiness in her friend's eyes spoke volumes. Since Aubrey married Connor over two years ago, the closeness of the friendship between her and Rachel had diminished. They had drifted apart. Aubrey wished she knew what was happening with Rachel.

Cooper burped. She wiped the baby's mouth. Her son was fighting sleep, but when he yawned, she could see his irises. He had Connor's blue eyes.

Kim stood in front of Leslie and asked, "What's next?"

"The inside's almost finished. I usually loop garland on the railings outside. Would you two mind decorating the outside while we finish in here?"

Rachel's smile was sad. *Why?* "Sure. We'll take care of it."

Before Rachel could move, Kim retrieved her coat and held it for her. Kim's attentiveness toward Rachel reminded Aubrey of Connor. *I'm so lucky.* Connor treated Aubrey like a queen.

Leslie's giggle caught Aubrey's attention. Leslie and Isaac were finishing the miscellaneous interior decorations. Right now, the pair were hanging wreaths on the inside of the windows. Isaac had his arm through a number of wreaths as they walked to the living room window.

Leslie hung one on a hooked suction cup. "How's that look? Is it pretty?"

Isaac had a strange look on his face as he studied Leslie. "Yes. But I know of a sight that's even more beautiful."

Leslie's eyes were sparkling. "Really? What's that?"

Isaac gently placed one of the wreaths on top of Leslie's head, and then backed away. He pulled out his cell, snapped a picture and then displayed the screen to her. "Aubrey, look at this. I found the perfect Christmas present."

Leslie was laughing. One thing about it, Isaac's presence was keeping her sister-in-law pre-occupied. *More than pre-occupied, she's glowing.* Maybe it was Aubrey's imagination, but Leslie appeared to be happier than Aubrey had seen her act the whole time Leslie dated Joe.

The pair were snickering as they continued to decorate the windows. Aubrey's mind drifted back to the night when Leslie confessed to her about the stolen kisses with Isaac. And what Leslie told her she saw in Isaac's eyes. *"Everything I ever wanted."* Aubrey couldn't help but giggle.

"Hey, what are you laughing about?" Connor asked.

She kept her voice low. "Did you see what's happening over there?"

Connor leaned in and kissed her cheek. "You mean my sister and your brother?"

"Yeah, that's it."

"And this amuses you?"

"Actually, no. I was thinking about what your sister says all the time."

"About me attending a university and—"

"No, no. Not that. She's always saying everything happens for a reason. Remember?"

His smile was wide. "Yes. I remember her lecturing me on that subject more than once." His blue eyes were inquisitive and seemed to go on forever. "And you're thinking of the things that happened to bring these two together?"

"You got it."

Connor shook his head. "Let's hope not."

Aubrey turned and immediately saw the twinkle in his eye. *Here it comes.* "Why wouldn't we want them to be together?"

"Because I refuse to stop kissing you. I want you to know that up front."

"What are you talking about now?"

"If those two get married, you won't just be my wife… you'll be my sister."

"Sister-*in-law*. I believe the marriage trumps the in-law part."

He was trying hard not to laugh. "Only in a few states."

A loud crash came from the kitchen. "Momma?" Grey's voice quivered like it did when she was about to cry. All four adults rushed into the kitchen.

Grey was standing next to the counter. An empty box rested upside down next to a pile of broken ceramic pieces. The debris covered the floor in front of Grey. "I'm sorry. I only wanted to look at it, but it fell and broke."

Leslie squatted down to survey the damage. "Is this the antique nativity set? The thing you dropped?"

Tears formed in Grey's eyes "I didn't mean it. I'm sorry."

Leslie shook her head. "Don't worry about it." Her tone didn't match her words.

Connor held Grey and patted her back. "It will be fine, honey. Everyone knows you didn't do it on purpose. Isn't that right, Aunt Leslie?"

Leslie sighed. "Of course not, sweetie. It's okay. It's just a thing. You're what's important." Leslie hugged Grey for a long second.

Aubrey whispered, "We'll pay for a new one."

"Thanks, but I'm not sure where I'll find another one of those."

Isaac also knelt, picking through the bigger pieces. "What was this?"

"It was a 1951 Hummel Goebel nativity scene."

Isaac whistled. "Wow. That's kind of rare, isn't it?"

She nodded. "Even rarer, now. I have no idea where I'd even begin looking for another one. I found that one in New York City."

He stood and offered Leslie his hand. "Oh ye of little faith. We'll find one. You know, it's a good thing I'm here to help you. If you're not busy tomorrow, we'll begin our quest in New Oxford. How's that sound?"

Leslie's eyes lit up. "New Oxford?"

Isaac nodded. "Antique capital of the world. You game?"

"Sure. What time?"

"How about I pick you up at seven and we'll go out for breakfast on the way. There's this diner just off Route 30 on the Manheim Pike I've heard about."

If Leslie smiled any wider, her teeth would surely fall out.

The pair returned to the living room while Connor grabbed a broom and a dust pan. "And once again, I find my wife can see the future."

"What do you mean?"

He dumped the crumbled remains of the statues in the garbage before turning to face Aubrey. "What you said earlier."

"Connor, stop talking in riddles."

"Something you said a few minutes ago. It explains why the nativity set got broken. You know, everything happens for a reason."

***

Kim knocked at the door a little after nine. He'd dropped Rachel off late last evening when they'd finished decorating at Connor and Aubrey's home. The women had been too tired to have the slumber party they talked about. *Are you in there?* It seemed to be taking forever for her to answer. *Maybe something's wrong.*

Kim tried calling her phone, but there was no answer. *Did she leave with Leslie and Isaac?* Her car was still parked outside.

Kim's shoulders tensed. *Now what do I do?* Part of his mind said he should just walk away. Rachel didn't seem to be very interested in his company last night. Her mind was certainly elsewhere. Probably on her ex-fiancé. In any case, she'd been depressed.

The buzzing of an ultra-light aircraft overhead drew his attention. It was probably flying out of the small airport in Smoketown. *The one Jenna dubbed*

'Smoketown International'. He climbed into his car, preparing to leave when the thought struck him. He remembered the depth of the pain on the really bad days. *Suppose the depression got to be too much?* Rachel might need help. Kim climbed out of the car again, this time with the intent of kicking the door in.

He started up the ramp when the neighing of a horse floated on the wind toward him—the horse from the neighboring property. *Connor and Aubrey's house. Maybe she's there.* Kim once again jumped in his vehicle and covered the short distance to the old farmhouse. He ran onto the porch and pounded on the door with his fist.

Aubrey answered. "Good morning, Kim. What's up?"

"I hate to bother you, but do you know where Rachel is?"

Aubrey glanced past him to Leslie's house. "Her car's there. What, didn't she answer?"

"No. And she didn't answer my call either. I'm concerned about her."

"It does seem peculiar."

"Did you notice how depressed she was last night?"

Aubrey's brows furrowed, and then she nodded. "Let me get my coat. I have a house key, so I'll just slip inside to see if she's okay."

"Thank you."

Aubrey asked Connor to stay with the children while she investigated.

Fear for Rachel's safety was building and seemed to be ready to boil over. "Do you mind if I tag along?"

"No. That sounds like a really good idea."

Aubrey slipped her key into the lock, and then pushed the door open slowly. "Rachel? It's Aubrey. Are you in here?" They looked in the downstairs, but there was nothing unusual. Aubrey led the way to the second floor. Rachel now occupied the bedroom where Connor used to stay.

Kim spoke, more so to hear noise. "I hope she's okay."

"Me, too." Aubrey pushed open the door. "Rach, are you okay?" Silence greeted them. The room seemed to be in perfect order, except the unmade bed. Aubrey walked to the bedside table. "Here's her phone. Maybe she went for a walk."

"We were supposed to go out for breakfast this morning."

"I'm sorry. You said she seemed rather melancholy yesterday. Do you know why?"

"I think so. She's stuck in the past, like I used to be." Glancing at Aubrey, he saw the question in her eyes. "The man who left her at the altar. He still has a grip on her heart. I know you two are friends. Did you know him?"

"No. In all the years I've known her, she never mentioned anything about that."

"It's hard, holding something like that inside. And until she confronts it, she won't get past it."

"Poor Rachel." Aubrey paused. "Do you want to wait over at our house for a while?"

Maybe I pushed too hard. "No. I think I can read the writing on the wall. Thanks for coming over to look. And thanks to your family for including me in your traditions. That was really fun."

After she relocked the house, Aubrey left. There was still no sign of Rachel. *Should I wait for her?* Kim's mind whispered to scratch the day off as a loss and leave, but his heart sent a different signal—to give her time and space and not force her along. He mulled the two arguments over in his mind before leaving a note for Rachel.

Standing on the porch, he searched the road for her one last time. Nothing. "I understand it, Rachel, I really do. But the next move... the next move is up to you."

***

Rachel was in the living room when a movement outside caught her attention. Walking to the window, she caught a glimpse of a shadow just before it slipped behind the bank barn. Bravely she stepped into the dark to investigate.

The night was black with no sign of the moon. Clouds hid the stars. Suddenly, a shuffling noise echoed from inside the barn. She reached for the door. It slowly swung outward.

Rachel was just about to enter when hands grabbed her arms, pulling her inside. Someone forced her body up against the stall. She struggled, but was no match for his power. A pair of lips found hers. Strong hands released her arms and moved to hold her face. "I've missed you, Rach."

"Eli? Is it really you?"

"Yes. I couldn't take it any longer. I came back for you."

"I missed you so much. I should have run away with you years ago."

"Will you come with me now?"

Without a second of hesitation, she answered, "Yes, yes."

He embraced her, lifting her body off the ground. "I've got a car waiting. This way."

Hand in hand, they ran toward his old red Chevy Nova. The one he'd had before he disappeared. Just before they reached the car, spotlights lit the night. The illumination was blinding.

A group of men approached from the shadows and surrounded them. One man stepped forward. "Come along peacefully and we won't have to hurt the girl."

She clung tightly to Eli's arm. "No, don't leave me again."

He softly kissed her lips. "I'm sorry, Rach. I think it's best if I go now."

Rachel tried to cling to him, but one of the men restrained her. The others shoved Eli into a van, closed the door and sped off.

The man who held her gently turned Rachel to face him. "It's time for Eli to return to his prison of exile. Don't make the same mistake and lock yourself into a cell of your own making. Live your life, be free." The man's face changed before her eyes and she recognized him immediately. The male who restrained her was Kim Landis.

Rachel jumped out of bed, soaked with sweat. The sky outside was beginning to show color in the east. Still in a daze, she glanced at the barn. Maybe it was her imagination, but she could have sworn a figure slipped around the corner. *Could it really be Eli?*

Quickly dressing, she ran outside, searching for the ghostly figure. When she reached the barn, she saw it again, scooting into a distant fence row on the Stoltzfus farm. Every time she got close, the form moved further and further away.

Her path took her across a creek. The cold water sent a shiver over her shoulders. *What am I doing?* This was the exact location where she'd seen the figure cross the creek, but there were no footprints. *This should be where he crossed.* But there was nothing there. Head down, Rachel suspected it had all been her imagination.

The house was growing closer as she walked through the cornfield. *Why do I torture myself with these lies?* Eli was never coming back. *And I'm tired of wallowing in self-pity.* She needed to find a way to get him out of her mind.

Rachel climbed the ramp to the porch and stared at the door. *Oh no!* She'd been in such a hurry to chase her dream this morning that she'd forgotten the housekey. Trying the door, her heart dropped further. It was locked.

"Now what do I do?" She could walk to Aubrey's house, but she'd probably have to confess how she'd locked herself outside. *Wait!* "Maybe Leslie keeps a key under the mat."

When she knelt, she saw it. There was a folded-up paper shoved partially under the door. She unraveled it. Rachel quickly recognized Kim's longhand.

Rachel,

Good morning or afternoon, depending on when you get this. I just hope you're okay. We were supposed to have breakfast together this morning, but I guess something came up. Maybe it was an accident, but then again, I think I've been pushing too hard. As you can see, I'm not very good at this romance stuff. I love you and heard you say the words, too, but maybe the only reason you said it was to try and please me. And it's entirely possible that I'm seeing something that's not there because that's what I wish to see. And maybe you are just too polite to tell me to take a hike.

Not knowing where we stand or how you feel, I'll leave the next step up to you. Don't worry, I promise the working relationship won't get all creepy no matter what you decide.

Thanks for listening,

Kim

P.S. I understand it, Rachel, I really do. But the next move... the next move is up to you.

Rachel allowed the paper to fall to the porch. "Oh, Kim. I don't want to hurt you."

***

Leslie couldn't help but stare at the man driving. It was actually kind of cool riding in his old Ford, though it smelled like the inside of a tire dealer's garage. Not offensive, but techy. *Devo's smell.* "So you work on cars?"

"I have my inspection license, but these days, I seem to spend most of my time working on pumps and heating systems and old John Deere tractors."

"What did you do before you came here?"

"I was a farm equipment mechanic. Didn't mind the work, but I hated the hours. You see, when it came time to harvest wheat or corn, I'd live out of my truck for days on end, following the combines."

Leslie was enjoying his profile. Despite the light jacket, his square shoulders impressed her. "Is that why you moved east?"

For the first time since he'd picked her up, his grin faded. "No. Like I said, it was a girl issue."

"I'm sorry."

"I'm not. I got to move in with my little sister and meet all you fine folk."

She felt playful and bold. "All of us, or maybe someone in particular?"

That smile was returning. He turned and shot a wink her way. "Maybe some more than others."

Leslie was hoping she could read his mind. *We'll come back to that later.* "You miss the Marines?"

"Mostly no. I think many of us who've left the Corps all feel the same. We have a love-hate relationship with the United States Marine Corps. We love reminiscing and bragging about our days as leathernecks, but I don't really believe we'd go back. Let me tell you, Leslie, when people started shooting at me, my fun meter was kind of tapped out."

He was funny. "This truck's in good shape for as old as it is. Are you going to get a new one soon?"

Isaac cleared his throat. "To a civilian like you, it appears to be an old truck. However, this is a classic. You, my friend, are riding in a 1997 F-150 XLT extended cab. You see, '97 was when Ford introduced the new rounded body style. It was *Motor Trend's* truck of the year."

"I know. I had one, like twenty years ago." She couldn't help it. She started giggling. "But then I grew up, moved onwards and upwards."

He joined her laughter. "If you think getting a Chevy was an upgrade... I'll stop now before I offend you. Unless you're talking a '69 Camaro SS. That's the ultimate classic car."

Her mouth was suddenly dry. "Really? Is that your all-time favorite?"

He nodded. "Yep. What's yours?"

"A '69 Camaro RS/SS, Daytona Yellow."

"Wow. I preferred the LeMans Blue myself. But you've made a good point. I loved the hidden lights on the RS package. You got good taste. Somehow, I never would have suspected you were so well versed on classic cars."

"Surprised you, did I?" She flipped a wink at him. "You know, if you're a good boy, I just might have a few other surprises in store for you." As soon as the words left her mouth, her face caught fire. *I just flirted with him!*

He was nibbling on his lip, trying not to laugh. He turned off of Route 30. "Looks like we're here."

The ex-Marine parked in front of what looked to be an old factory. Isaac jumped out and opened her door. When he offered his arm, Leslie slid hers through the crook of his elbow. Despite their jackets, the firmness of his muscles rubbed against her skin. A lightness began in her chest. They strolled into the shop, which had rows and rows of treasures of yesteryear. *Few men his age collect antiquities.* "How long have you been collecting antiques?"

Turning his face to hers, he smiled. And it happened again. Just like that night... when he helped decorate the barn... and she couldn't control herself. She had kissed him.

"Actually, I don't own a single one. I just like to look, that's all. How about you?"

"I started a few years ago. That nativity set Grey dropped was the first one. I know she didn't mean it, but I loved that grouping. Looking at it, it took me back to a place in time when things were much simpler."

"I feel the same way, akin to taking a glimpse of history. Like living in a Norman Rockwell world."

Her entire body tingled. "How did you know?"

"Know what?"

"That's *exactly* how I feel and that's why I love antiquing. Did Connor tell you I've said the same thing in the past?"

"Uh-uh. That's just how I feel. Life was simpler back then. Kids had time to be kids. Families would sit down and eat meals together. It makes me sad in one respect." He stopped and picked up a trinket from the 1964 World's Fair. "I think our country has lost its innocence."

They walked in silence, but her arm remained entwined with his. *Can't believe I'm going to ask this, but I've got to know.* "Yesterday, you said you flirted with me that night. Why, and was it only a flirt, or...?"

He quit walking and turned her so they were facing. The warmth of his hands soothed her skin as he gripped her hands. "I don't play games, Leslie. You should know the truth. Since the day we met, I've been enchanted with you. To me, you're the prettiest girl I've ever met. Your eyes, your smile... I don't know what came over me that night, but I wanted to kiss you. No, I needed *you* to kiss me that evening."

"I seem to remember you kissing me, too."

His cheeks colored a little. "Yeah, but you kissed me first. After that, well..."

The thrill of his lips teased her memory. Her voice was barely a whisper. "Then why did you stop? Didn't you like it?"

He released her left hand and touched her cheek. "I needed to, for both our sakes. Never believed you'd actually kiss me, but I've got to tell you, Leslie, I think that was the best moment of my life."

Mine, too. "Then why'd you stop?"

"Because I respect you... and the relationship you had with the goofball." All of his face had now turned pink. "I hope you don't think less of me because of what I did. That was why I made myself scarce. I lost control and tempted you. Made a fool of myself. Can you forgive me?"

"That's not what I thought. I was afraid you believed I was a tramp, acting that way."

He shook his head, "You, a tramp? Never crossed my mind."

"Then I'll forgive you, but only if you forgive me." She stuck her hand out.

He smiled and shook with her. "Deal."

"So now what?"

He pulled her in, until their lips were almost touching. "Why don't we enjoy each other's company and see what God has in store for us?"

And just like the night they decorated her barn, she allowed her restraint to lapse. Leslie leaned forward and found his lips. Warm and wet, she lost track of the division in their bodies.

"Excuse me." Both of them tensed at the old woman's voice. "Can I give you a hand finding something special?"

Isaac winked at Leslie. "Thank you, ma'am, but I believe I already found what I've been looking for, all my life."

Chapter Twelve

R achel turned off the light and sneaked to the window of her classroom. The one that overlooked the faculty parking lot. And she saw him, head down as he walked to his car. Rachel shrank into the corner of her window. Kim hesitated before climbing in. His gaze seemed to take in her classroom, but only for a brief moment. The man closed the vehicle door and drove off into the night.

The refrigerator handle in the faculty room was world-class sticky. After retrieving her boxed meal for one, she scrubbed her hands. The kids would start arriving for practice in about an hour. Returning to her classroom, Rachel ate in silence. Kim was on her mind, as he had been since the last time they'd really spoken. The day before they'd missed breakfast. *I wish I would have driven over to his house and begged forgiveness.*

The alfredo noodles were chewy. *Should have bought the brand name, not the store brand.* The white sauce also seemed to be a little thin.

When she raised the water bottle to her lips, she felt it again. Someone's eyes on her. This seemed to happen every evening about this time. Feeling as if she were an actress in some perverted voyeur's dream, Rachel walked to the corner and ditched her food into the garbage. Acting as if she were leaving the room, she turned off the light. But as soon as she cleared the door frame, Rachel dropped to her knees and crawled back into the room. Making sure the hallway lights did not silhouette her, she slowly raised her head so she could look outside.

"There you are." All alone in the center of the parking lot, a tall man stood. Rachel couldn't be sure, but he seemed to be particularly interested in her room. Lights from a car entering the lot flowed toward his direction. As if a mirage, the man disappeared. *Just like the figure I saw outside that day.*

Rachel noted her hands were shaking. *Why would someone stalk me?* But it wasn't only here at school that she'd sensed him. Twice in the past week, she could have sworn someone had been lurking in the shadows near Leslie's bank barn.

She took one last peek outside. No, there was no one there. It was just her imagination. A voice whispered in her ear. *Or is it?*

***

Isaac carried the bouquet of roses in the bend of his arm as he covered the short distance to Leslie's house. Approaching on the other side of the road was a bicycle... and the girl who used to count him as a friend, Rebecca. These days, she didn't even give him the time of day. She rolled on past in the other direction without so much as a glance.

"What could I have done differently?" he muttered. Yes, he liked Rebecca, but with the vast difference in age, he'd never seriously considered a possible relationship between them. And there was the whole issue of being "plain." While he respected the Amish, he didn't agree with them turning their back on modern conveniences.

A motorcycle flew past him. Rebecca's face floated in front of him. The vision began with the smile from that night when they drove back from Green Dragon. Her face transitioned to rapture as they moved to kiss. Then like frost discolors a mum, Rebecca's face turned sour. Those last words echoed in his ears. *"It's late and I don't want anyone to get the wrong impression."* He'd not only lost a friend that night, he'd damaged a pure young heart.

The wind was stiff this evening. It was the first full week in December and the temperature was well below freezing. He started to pull his jacket tighter over his frame, but sudden thoughts of Leslie warmed him all over. They were having a game night tonight. She had shown him some of the old games she'd collected over the years—Rack-O, a vintage board game called Seven Seas, A Barrel of Monkeys and another board game called Cooties.

He laughed, deeply. It didn't matter what they did. He loved being with Leslie. *Can't believe my luck.* All spring, summer and fall, he'd fantasized what it would be like to spend time with her. And now, Leslie seemed to want to hang around with him all the time. *Better than my dreams.*

Before he realized it, Isaac was at her door. He didn't even have the chance to knock when it swung open. A smile split her lips and she wrinkled her nose at him. "Good evening, how was your day?"

"I can't seem to remember."

She giggled. "Why can't you remember?"

Isaac shifted to a southern accent. "Because, my little apple blossom, I'm all agog to be in your presence tonight. Since I saw your face, nothing else matters."

Her expression seemed to melt as she wrapped her arms around him. And much to his extreme pleasure, she kissed him deeply.

Leslie rubbed her nose against his and then backed away. "I missed you today."

"Missed you, too. Did you think about my proposition for the weekend?"

"I did, but let's eat supper first before we discuss plans. I made beef pot pie for dinner. Hope you're hungry."

Isaac's mouth started to water. "I've heard tales of your legendary pot pie. You know, your brother takes cracks at everything about you, except your cooking."

"Really? Aubrey's a pretty good cook. Being the kind, loving and devoted husband he pretends to be, I wouldn't be surprised if he tells your sister her cooking is better than mine."

Isaac followed her into the kitchen and lifted the crock pot onto the table. The tasty aroma made his stomach grumble. Leslie already had the table set, as well as two tapered candles, which were lit. "May I get your seat?"

Those blue eyes beckoned to him. "Yes. I know my brother likes my cooking. What about you?"

"It's fantastic. But I have a confession to make and don't be angry."

Leslie's smile faded and her eyes seemed to dim. "You're scaring me. Last time you made a confession, you punched someone."

He couldn't contain the chuckle. "No punches this time, I promise."

"Good. What is it?"

"I think I upset my sister. I was raving about the fried chicken you made the other night, and well, she got a little angry."

"Aubrey, mad? There had to be some other reason."

"I think she'd have been okay if it hadn't been for Connor."

Leslie's eyes opened wide. "What did my dumb brother say now?"

"He told me no one else in the world makes fried chicken as good as you. I really think he hurt Aubrey's feelings."

Leslie shook her head. "That boy's not the brightest. Connor should be nicer to his wife. She's the best thing to ever happen to him." Her smile drew him in. "Mind if I say the prayer tonight?"

"No, go ahead."

She reached across the table and took his hand. "Father, we thank You for the bounty before us tonight. We thank You for our families and how blessed we are." Isaac noted her hand trembling slightly. "And this may be a little audacious, but... we know You are in control of everything. We understand everything happens for a reason. And Lord, I know You know my heart, my desires, my wishes. I ask You to bless us tonight, to show us your way for our lives."

Leslie grew quiet. Isaac filled the silence. "And teach us, Lord, Your way. Show us how to be friends, to respect each other, to really get to know each other. And if it be Your way, help us to build a deep closeness that is pleasing in your eyes."

He waited for Leslie, to see if she wanted to add to the prayer. He peeked and saw her smile. She whispered, "Amen. Thank you, Devo."

"For what?"

"For being respectful. For caring about me. For having the ability to be able to finish my sentences. I, I think I might be—"

A crashing noise interrupted them.

Leslie's eyes grew wide. "What in the world was that?"

He was already up and moving. Isaac threw open the door and ran toward the trash cans which were on their side. One was still rolling, its trash overflowing onto the lawn. Leslie followed two steps behind him.

Isaac stood, silent as a tree. His head slowly rotated as he searched the night.

Leslie's voice was slightly louder than a whisper. "Could it have been the wind?"

"No."

"Maybe a coyote? Connor told me he's seen one a couple of times."

"Only if the coyote wears size eleven dress shoes."

Leslie eyed him strangely. "What?"

He held up a brown loafer. "I'm afraid your garbage can had a visitor."

***

Kim slipped in to take the last available chair. The principal had announced an emergency staff meeting minutes before the last period ended. Glancing around the room, his eyes fell on Rachel. She was seated between Laurie Folkenroth, the biology teacher and Bob Snyder, algebra. Bob's eyes were on Rachel, but Rachel's eyes were focused on the floor.

What can I do to help her? He'd pondered that quite a bit. Maybe he had it all wrong. Perhaps it had nothing to do with him at all.

Dr. Wilson walked into the room and closed the door behind him. "I thank everyone for accommodating me this afternoon on such short notice. The reason I asked you to stay later this evening is to discuss a potential security threat. There have been multiple reports of a strange man lurking around the parking lot after dark. Security reviewed the history on the camera system and confirmed the reports."

Kim was watching Rachel's reaction. Her face was pale and her mouth was hanging open. She seemed to be hanging on Wilson's every word.

"We've consulted with both the local and state police. Starting tonight, there will be a heavier than normal law enforcement presence." The principal turned and appeared to be speaking directly to Rachel. "We will also have additional security in the parking lot both an hour before and an hour after play rehearsals. Continued, enhanced security protocols will be in place every evening until the play is finished. Ms. Domitar, please make sure we release the students on time each night."

"Yes sir, Dr. Wilson."

"Thank you. Any questions?"

Bev Barker, the physical education teacher raised her hand. "Do you have a description of this man?"

Wilson pulled a paper from his pocket. "Unfortunately, we weren't able to get a whole lot of detail. The police estimate the suspect is Caucasian and approximately six foot tall. He has a mustache and was seen wearing a dark blue hoodie and light blue jeans. Any other questions?"

Ms. Folkenroth raised her hand next. "Do we know why he's out there? I mean, have there been any threats or anything?"

"No. There have been no threats that we're aware of. Any guess as to the man's purpose would be a supposition at best."

Rachel appeared to be quite shaken. When the meeting broke up, Kim waited for her. He noticed her hands were trembling. "Are you doing all right?"

She motioned for him to stay. After all the other educators left, Rachel faced him. "I think this whole ordeal has something to do with me."

"What?"

"A couple of times this week, I thought I saw someone lurking around Leslie's barn. I assumed it was my imagination. And then two nights ago, someone knocked over her garbage cans."

"Could it have been the wind or an animal?"

She shook her head. "No. Isaac found an abandoned man's shoe and footprints, one shoe on, one missing. He tracked it across the fields, but didn't catch the guy."

Kim touched her arm. "Who do you think it is?"

Rachel hesitated. "I, I don't know." Her cheeks turned red. *She's scared.*

"That settles it. I'll hang around and personally walk you out to your car tonight."

"That's kind of you, but I don't want to impose."

"Nonsense. I'll also follow you home and make sure you get in the house safely."

Rachel's eyes seemed glued to his. Her next words were whispered. "Why would you do that, after how I've ignored and treated you?"

Because I'm in love with you. "It's okay. Please don't misread my intentions. There are no strings attached. I'm just trying to help you out and make sure you get home without harm."

She winced. "Kim, I'd like to say I'm sorry about—"

"Stop it. The only thing you need to worry about tonight is the play, okay?"

"I, I don't know what to say, except... thank you."

He smiled. "That's what friends do."

She reached for his hand and then squeezed it. "You're a wonderful man and a great friend. Thank you. You have no idea how much safer this makes me feel."

"Good. I'll be at the back of the auditorium, waiting. Sound okay?"

"Kim, I know I haven't treated you—"

He put his finger to her lips. "Just concentrate on the play."

"Wait. Can we talk about this?"

I'd love that, but... "We can, just not right now. It's almost time for the rehearsal and I don't want to distract you. But I promise, when you're ready to discuss it, I will be too."

A smile filled her face. "Okay. I'll be on stage." She walked down the hallway, but stopped and turned to face him. "And you're waiting for me, right?"

"Yes, just take as much time as you need." Rachel smiled and turned away from him. *I'll be here, even if you take forever.*

Chapter Thirteen

"Doesn't the snow make everything look so clean and fresh?" Isaac was escorting Leslie down the ramp to her vehicle. Perhaps two inches of snow covered the grassy areas.

She surveyed the white covered landscape. Leslie stopped and turned so they were facing one another. "I love when it snows. I'm dreaming of a white Christmas, you know?"

"The movie, the song or the real thing?"

"Do I only get to choose one?"

He kissed her hand. "The world's the limit and nothing can stop you. If you can dream it, you can do it. And I plan on helping to make your dreams come true."

She opened her arms and he met her halfway. Her voice was just a whisper. "What did I do before I met you?"

"I don't know, but I wouldn't want to ever find out." He kissed her gently. "Shall we go?"

Isaac helped her into the driver's seat of the Suburban. Leslie had insisted on driving today. They were still on their quest for that 1951 Nativity set. Today, they were heading to Lewisburg, the home of

Bucknell University. The town had a number of antique shops.

"Now, admit it. Isn't my Suburban a lot more comfortable than your old pickup?"

Isaac had found that one thing Leslie loved to do was tease him. He decided to give it back to her. "I guess, but I miss the ambiance of my faithful companion."

"Ambiance? You mean the smell?"

"Aww, don't be a hater."

"Hmm, your comment gives me a perfect idea for a gift for you this season."

"And that would be?"

She pulled out of the drive and headed in a northerly direction. "An air freshener that smells like a garage." Leslie had quipped that was what his truck smelled like.

"I love that smell. Can you get a couple of them? Maybe so they can mask that pumpkin spice odor in your house."

"Smartie. Look, here comes your friend." Leslie pointed to an open-topped buggy that was heading toward them.

He recognized the girl. *Rebecca*. There was a young Amish man driving that Isaac hadn't seen before. Isaac raised his hand to acknowledge them, but the two young people stared straight ahead.

"I was wondering when that would happen."

"When what would happen?"

"When she'd finally start dating. She would have to be in her late twenties."

"Rebecca's eighteen."

Leslie whipped her head to stare at him. "You answered that awfully quick. What, are you the official historian on Becky Stoltzfus?"

He could feel his face warming. "She doesn't like that name. She prefers Rebecca, and no. We only work together."

Leslie's eyes were on the road, mainly. Her voice was no longer jovial. "If that's true, then why'd she invite *you* to Thanksgiving dinner?"

Aubrey had warned him Leslie would bring this up someday. "You know much about her grandmother?"

"Not really. When I first bought this place, I tried to be sociable. One evening when I was out for a walk, I stopped by to say hello. Old Mrs. Stoltzfus was aloof. Know what she told me?"

"No."

"She told me that good fences made good neighbors."

He unzipped his jacket. The heater was warming up. "Was she intentionally being rude?"

"I'm not sure. At first I thought it was a reference to the Robert Frost poem, *The Mending Wall*, but I think she really meant that as neighbors, we should mind our own business."

"Wow. I never would have suspected she'd act that way."

"Do you know the old woman well?"

"No. Rebecca told me that her grandmother used to be English, but converted."

The smile that usually graced Leslie's face was missing. "Sounds like you know Rebecca purty gut, huh? Will you be taking your Christmas dinner over there as well?"

Rebecca's face flashed before his eyes. He shook his head to drive the sight away. "I'm... pretty sure I'm no longer welcome in their home."

The big Chevy shimmied when Leslie focused her attention on him. "Why? What happened?"

"The reason her father invited me over was to explain their customs... and how a man, dispositioned to do such, could convert from being English into their faith."

Leslie's teeth were gritted together and she muttered something under her breath.

"What did you say?"

"Don't worry about it." It was easy to see Leslie was upset.

He sighed. "Why do I get the feeling you're angry at me?"

"I'm not angry at you. I'm angry at... at her."

"Rebecca or her grandmother?"

"Whichever one's behind the plot."

Leslie's anger was real, but so was something else—her beauty. The fiery blue of her eyes was so intriguing. "What plot are you talking about?"

"That girl. She wants you to convert so she can have you, doesn't she?"

Isaac's mouth dropped open. "How did you know?"

Her breath was coming in short bursts, like a tea pot that's about ready to start whistling. "I just knew it." She pointed her vehicle into a long farm lane and threw the lever into park. Leslie shifted so she could face him.

"Devo, I need to know what happened. Exactly what went on."

"You're mad at me?"

"No, but... Look, this might be hard for you to understand, but... I've been hurt twice in my life. So... humor me, please. If there's ever going to be a chance for you and me, I need your honesty. Above all else. Now, what happened?"

His mind drifted back to his last romance. "I want to say something before I tell you. I was also hurt by dishonesty. Because of that, I try my best to always be truthful, but for you..." Isaac hesitated, looking for the right word. "I never want any secrets between us. Ever. I think the world of you, Leslie."

"As I do you."

"Okay, the full truth. Her father invited me over, but I'm pretty sure it was at the direction of the grandmother. I thought they were being polite, telling me about their ways. The day after Thanksgiving, I think I discovered the real reason. Rebecca and I tended market together, all day. I could tell something was different about her."

"And that was?"

"I don't know... like maybe the formal wall between us had been lowered a little."

Leslie had her arms crossed, head leaned back against the seat as she watched him. "In other words, more intimate?"

"No, not like that. She joked with me and called me by my first name, not 'English' or 'Golden'. Then on the way home, she asked if I would consider converting."

"Because she wanted you?"

He nodded. "Yes. She told me she wanted me to be her husband. When I told her I wouldn't convert, she told me she'd leave the faith for me. She was willing to leave her family and become like me, English."

Leslie's eyes changed. Sorrow but understanding. "She really loves you."

He ignored her comment. He wanted to reassure her. "I told her there was too much of an age difference, that it wouldn't work out. And that's when it happened."

Her eyes grew large. "What happened?"

"She kissed me. When I said we couldn't do that anymore, she said if I kissed her like we were in love, and could still say no, she'd leave me alone."

"Did you kiss her?"

He nodded. "Yep."

Leslie turned away. She was biting her lip and nodding her head. Trying hard to fight back a sob.

"Before I could say a word, she looked away. Rebecca knew, without me saying it."

Leslie's brows arched. "What did she know?"

Moment of truth. "That my heart belonged to somebody else."

She cocked her head. "Somebody else? Whom might that be?"

He lightly touched her face. "I hope you know by now. It's you, and has been since the day we met."

***

Rachel smiled as Kim closed the door of the Honda for her. Since the meeting with the principal, he'd patiently waited each night at the back of the auditorium, followed her home and walked her to safety, inside Leslie's house. But this night was going to be different. After the faculty meeting, she'd asked if they could talk about their relationship. He'd agreed, but told her to concentrate on rehearsals first. Kim said he was in no hurry, he didn't mind waiting. And this evening, she wanted to make things right between them.

No sooner had she guided the vehicle from the lot when the phone rang. A smile graced her lips when she recognized the caller ID. The warmth filling her chest was a sharp contrast to the freezing cold interior. *Kim.* Not to appear over-eager, she allowed it to ring three times before accepting the call on hands-free. "Hey there."

"Hi, Rach. Is it ever cold out here tonight? My dash says it's fourteen."

"Wow, that's freezing. Hey, I was kind of hoping, uh, like maybe you could stop in for a few minutes tonight and stay a while. You promised we could talk after rehearsals and, since this evening was our last one..."

She could hear his sigh, and it seemed happy. "I'm looking forward to that. But first, I need to make an announcement, about the play. Something the principal asked me to tell you, but not until after all the rehearsals were finished."

A tingling feeling walked across her shoulders. "Okay. What's that?"

"Do you know Didi Phillips-Zinn?"

"Yes, that name is familiar. Wait. Isn't she the newscaster for the Harrisburg television station? Why would you ask about her?"

"Well, she apparently heard about the play... and... are you ready for this?"

Her hands were now shaking. "Yes."

"Sitting down?"

"Of course, silly. I'm driving. What is it? Tell me, Kim."

Kim cleared his throat. "It seems no other district in the area has ever performed this play, and it apparently holds a special place in the newscaster's heart. Ms. Zinn has convinced her station to video the show. They plan to broadcast it as a special event on Christmas Eve. I've been told Didi wants to interview you, as sort of a director's cut, so you can add commentary while it's being televised." Her eyes blurred and she could hear the emotion in his voice. "I am so, so proud of you, my friend. Your enthusiasm is contagious. The kids worship you. The parents love you. The school staff respects you. Even the school board has taken notice of your impact. And now, the local community will get to see the rewards of your labor. And, and how wonderful you are. Thank you, Rachel."

She had to wipe her cheeks. "Thank me? For what?"

"For being the most amazing woman... I've *ever* met."

"I can't take the full credit. None of this would have been possible, not without your help and support."

He snickered across the airwaves. "And our story... I remember those voice mails you left me, about interviewing for the job. I knew you were special even then."

Her chest was on fire. She had to unbutton her coat. "Really, like how special?"

"I've, uh, never met anyone who has the ability to move me like you do. It's been a while since I've said it, but... I love you, Rachel."

It was her turn to laugh. Again, she wiped her coat sleeve across her cheeks. "I love you, too. Tonight, I'd like to explain what happened a couple of weeks ago. And apologize. I hope you'll forgive me."

Kim's voice was low. "No need to apologize. I'll gladly listen, but only if you want to tell me. Believe me, I understand. It's been five years since I lost Jenna, and thoughts of her have dominated my world since I found out she'd died. But in the last couple of months, something changed that has made the world bright again."

Her heart caught in her throat. *Me?* "And that would be?"

He didn't hesitate, not one second. "You."

***

Aubrey entered the Tea Room. The essence of pine and cinnamon seemed to compete for her attention. Sophie, the owner, welcomed her with that charming British accent. "Aubrey, it's so great to see you again. Merry Christmas."

"Merry Christmas to you as well. Are you ready for the big day?"

Sophie glowed as she led her to the table. "Yes. This will be a special Christmas." The petite blonde patted her stomach. "Found out yesterday I'm expecting, again. I surely hope it's a girl this time. Benjy and I have three sons already."

"Wow! Three kids? How do you manage? Cooper and Grey take all of my energy as it is."

"With lots of love." She stopped at the table where Leslie was already seated. "Here you are. Enjoy."

Leslie stood and hugged her. "You look tired, sis."

Aubrey nodded. "It's been a hectic week. Connor and I finished wrapping Grey's gifts at two this morning. We have to be extra careful where we hide the presents because the little stinker has turned out to be a big snoop."

Leslie shook her head. "Just like Connor." She pointed across the room. "Did you see our friend, the celebrity? She's meeting with that television woman this morning."

Aubrey glanced across the room. Rachel and Didi Phillips-Zinn were seated at a window table. A camera man was filming their discussion. "I've seen Didi in here before. Rumor has it she lives in Paradise. You know, I'm kind of envious. She always looks so pretty."

Leslie sniffed and Aubrey turned her attention to her sister-in-law. "And she always has such a sweet and genuine smile. You'd never know her husband is missing in action."

Aubrey again glanced at the other table. "Such a shame. My heart goes out to her."

Rachel and Ms. Zinn stood and embraced before the newscaster left. Rachel walked over and sat down. Leslie pulled a pen from her pocket. "Excuse me, Ms. Domitar. Could I have your autograph?"

Rachel's face turned pink. "Stop it."

Aubrey couldn't resist picking on her. "This is nice, you taking time to visit with us peasants."

Rachel shook her head and rolled her eyes. "The same goes for you, Aubrey Grace. Would you like to hear what the news lady and I talked about or do you want to pick on me instead?"

Leslie's face was filled with mirth. "Isn't that why we came?"

For the next ten minutes, Rachel talked about the interview. "I can't believe they're airing it on Christmas Eve."

"We can all watch it, right after the meal. I mean, you are both coming to our Christmas Eve party, aren't you?"

Rachel wrinkled her nose. "That depends."

"On what?"

"On whether I can invite Kim or not."

Aubrey's chest warmed. "Are you two back together?"

They had to wait until after Rachel finished her sip of tea. "Yes. In a big, big way."

Aubrey winked at her friend, then glanced at Leslie. "And of course you will be sitting next to my brother, Isaac, right?"

Leslie's eyes popped open wide. "Next to him? I was hoping to sit on his lap." The three of them laughed out loud.

Rachel's voice was subdued. "There's something purely magical about this place and time. I never dreamed I'd have a family this close or a love so real." She shifted her gaze between Aubrey and Leslie. "Thank you both. It wouldn't have been possible without the two of you."

Aubrey reached for her hand. "I'm not sure if it's the place or what. I feel like my life hadn't really begun until I moved here, you know, after my accident."

Leslie stood and curtsied before sitting back down. "You're both welcome. I know the credit all belongs to me. I mean, without me, Aubrey and Connor would have never fallen in love and Rachel never would have met Kim."

Aubrey laughed. "And here I thought Connor got it on his own. But now I know he learned it from his big sister."

Leslie turned to her. "Learned what?"

"Delusions of grandeur."

Again, all three of them laughed. Aubrey changed the subject. "Isaac told me he found footprints in the snow around your house again the other night."

Leslie's face clouded. "I don't understand that. Why would anyone have any interest in my house? It's not like I'm rich."

Rachel piped up. "Makes me feel creepy. I'm so glad Kim follows me home each night."

Leslie winked at Aubrey. "That's only so you two can make out on the porch for twenty minutes."

"Don't be jealous. It's not like you and Devo don't do it. When I come home, it seems you two are always cuddled up in front of the TV, binge watching Hallmark."

"And don't forget sharing my stash of pistachios."

Aubrey shook her head. "Hi. Let me introduce myself. I'm Aubrey Lapp." The other two women giggled. She transferred her gaze to Rachel. "Have there been any more sightings at the school?"

Rachel shook her head. "Not with the enhanced security. The thought of someone being out there, watching, unnerves me."

Aubrey nodded. "I know. We don't let Grey go outside to play by herself anymore. Connor always goes with her now. Grey appreciates it, as does Connor, mainly because he's getting out of work."

Leslie added, "Well, I for one feel much safer since Connor and Devo installed that security system. It's a little frustrating that we haven't picked up anything on the cameras. It's almost like whoever is out there knows where the cameras are pointed." She patted Aubrey's hand. "I'm glad they installed a similar system at your house."

Me, too. "It also makes me feel better knowing we've got a former Marine living with us."

Rachel smiled at Aubrey. "I believe Leslie would feel better if he lived with her."

Leslie playfully smacked Rachel's arm. "I'm not that kind of girl. He'd have to put a wedding ring on my hand before he does that."

Aubrey couldn't resist. "I'm sure my brother feels the same way. How's he say it?" She lowered her voice. "Always faithful, to God, family and the Corps."

All three of them added, "Oo-rah."

***

Isaac was tightening the battery clamps on the utility vehicle when he heard the door open. Looking up, he couldn't help but smile. His boss, Henry Campbell, was dressed in a red coat and cap with white trim. The fake beard almost made Isaac laugh. Hanging on his arm was his wife, Ellie. She sported a matching red and white Santa cape and cap over her classy, red velvet dress.

Henry extended his hand and handed Isaac an envelope. "Merry Christmas. Here's a little something to express our gratitude."

Isaac pulled off his hat. "Thank you. This was unexpected. Merry Christmas, boss." He turned to the girl with the twin dimples and glistening brown eyes. "And to you, Mrs. Campbell."

She curtsied. "Thank you. Are you ready for Christmas?"

"Just about. I ordered my last gift this morning. It was hard to find. Took me almost a month to locate it. And how about your family?"

Henry's eyes crinkled. "It will be another year of princesses and ponies. But that may change soon."

That's odd. "Come again?"

Ellie replied. "Henry's making reference to the fact he has three daughters and sorely wants a son." She patted her tummy. "Guess we'll have to see if this one is the son he wants or daughter number four."

Four? I haven't even thought about children. "Congratulations."

Henry replied for them. "Thanks. I don't know if you're interested, but Sophie Miller holds a cancer fundraiser on Christmas Eve at her Tea Room. Our company picks up the tab for admission for our employees, with or without a guest, if you'd like to attend. Are you interested in joining us?"

These people were so nice. "I appreciate it, but my sister holds a little get together on Christmas Eve. I kind of promised her I'd be there."

Ellie smiled. "We understand. Family always comes first. If for some reason you change your mind, feel free to join us. It starts at five and is usually over by ten. Merry Christmas, Isaac." Much to his surprise, the lady gave him a quick hug, then headed out the door.

Henry remained. "I wanted to let you know, twice in the last week I've discovered the Fuhrman brothers on my property. I kindly escorted them off the first time. The second, I gave them a little something to remind them I wasn't happy. Told them if it happens again, I'd call the police."

Isaac was pretty sure he could read between the lines. "What did you give them, sir?"

There was a fire in those Scottish eyes. "As a fellow ex-Marine, I'm sure you can imagine what I did when I found them harassing one of our female workers. Gave them an early Christmas present, if you know what I mean. Men do not talk to women that way or treat them like they were saying. At least not real men."

"Which one of our employees was it, sir? I'll keep an eye out."

"Rebecca. Rebecca Stoltzfus."

Chapter Fourteen

R achel's heart was in her throat. *Please let this go off without a major disaster.* The Friday night performance would soon begin. She took a quick peek through the curtain. The auditorium was packed. When she'd passed the cafeteria earlier, every seat had been full. The principal had told her that area sold out so quickly they'd opened up the gym where the show would be broadcast courtesy of the school's A/V Department.

"Rachel?" It was Didi Phillips-Zinn. The beautiful blonde stood before her. "Are you excited?"

"Hi. I'm more nervous than excited. Suppose it doesn't go well?"

"Aww, it'll be fine." The other woman searched her face. "Are you a God-fearing woman?"

What an odd question at a time like this. "Yes. Why?"

"Would it be okay if I prayed with you?"

"Uh, sure. I mean, please? I could use the help."

Didi offered her hand. Rachel took it. "Father in Heaven, today is an exciting day, not only for my friend Rachel, but also for all those involved in the play. We ask You to help everyone do their best and also ask You to open up the hearts of those who are watching... Allow them to feel Your spirit and know that wherever they are in their journey in life, You are always there. I ask a special blessing on my friend, Rachel. Keep her well, keep her sane and above all, let her know You are there and everything will be fine. Amen."

Rachel glanced at the news lady. The blonde smiled at her. "Thank you."

"Good luck. Break a leg." The younger woman quickly walked away.

"Ms. Domitar?" It was one of the student assistants. "Mr. Landis asked you to meet him in the faculty lounge. He told me to tell you it was important, but not urgent."

"Thanks." *Must be extremely important if Kim sent a runner for me.* She headed down the hall until she stood before the room.

Opening the door, a hand reached out and gently drew her into the dark room. The man softly closed the door and pulled her to him. Kim's face was so close, the warmth of his breath caressed her cheeks. "Before the craziness starts, I wanted to take a moment and wish you good luck. I'm so proud of you." His lips found hers and the world seemed to melt away.

When they finally broke off, she had to hold tightly to his arms to maintain her balance. "Thank you."

He kissed her again, but briefly. "I love you. Now, go conquer the world!"

Kim walked next to her as if nothing had happened, but it had. Despite all the zillions of things that were competing for her attention, the only thing that seemed to matter was the tingling of her lips. From Kim's kiss.

Before she realized it, he led her to a location that was just behind the curtain on the stage and then Kim departed. The lights flickered on and off twice.

Rachel recognized the voice of the principal, Dr. Wilson. "Greetings everyone. Happy Holidays. I would like to welcome you to our school and our presentation of *It's a Wonderful Life*. As the saying goes, it takes a village, so I'd like to dedicate a few moments to thank those who have made tonight possible." For the next two minutes, Wilson rattled off name after name.

"And of course, tonight wouldn't be possible without the vision, enthusiasm and drive of our wonderful drama teacher, Ms. Rachel Domitar. Rachel, please come out and take a bow."

The curtain flew open and she walked on stage. A roar erupted to her left and she turned. Her mouth dropped open as she took in the stage, filled with not only the actors and actresses, but every person involved in the production. They were all applauding. A second even louder cheer rose behind her from the audience. To her utter disbelief, everyone was standing, clapping and shouting.

Two faces stuck out in the crowd. Kim was beaming as he smiled at her. On the other side of the auditorium, Didi Phillips-Zinn caught her attention. The news lady mouthed, "See?" and shot her two thumbs up.

It was over three minutes before the noise died down. Overwhelmed, Rachel swallowed hard. "Wow. I hope this show can measure up to your expectations." Heavy laughter. "This production isn't just my doing. Every cast member, stage hand, band member," she glanced at Kim, "faculty advisor and everyone else who contributed in any way had a hand in this." She sought out the smiling face of her friend, Didi, and shot a wink at her. "And may your hearts be opened to the true meaning behind this show." Didi made the motion of hugging herself and sending it to Rachel. "Ladies and gentlemen, without further ado, we present our version of *It's a Wonderful Life*."

***

Isaac grabbed a towel from his toolbox and wiped off the dirt from the knees of his jeans. Luckily, he'd been able to get parts overnighted from the west coast so he could replace the regulator on the propane tank. Without a functioning regulator, the gas wouldn't be able to flow properly to the heaters and the entire crop of strawberries would be in jeopardy. Not anymore. Isaac had replaced it and the system was up and running. Those strawberries were safe now.

It was almost ten on the final Saturday morning before Christmas. Isaac wanted to head into Lancaster and it was still early enough in the day that he could get there and back before Leslie and her mother returned from Philly and their shopping trip.

Isaac fired up his Ford and pointed it toward home. The gift he'd searched so long for had finally arrived yesterday. Now, he simply needed to locate the proper wrapping paper to go with it. But because his knees were filthy, Isaac wanted to change his pants before heading into town. While he was there, he might as well ask Grey if she would want to ride along. He loved the little girl and besides, Aubrey seemed to be exhausted lately. This might give his sister a break.

He had just turned onto the road where Aubrey lived when he saw it. An open-topped buggy was in the ditch and the horse was down, barely moving. Parked further down the road was a beat-up truck. Isaac steered off the road, jumped out and ran to the buggy. Immediately recognizing the young Amish man as the one escorting Rebecca a few days ago, Isaac noted the man's bloody nose and dazed look. He was now leaned against the partially overturned wagon.

Before Isaac could say a word, the man pleaded, "Help. Those men ran us off the road, into the ditch. I think my horse needs a doctor."

"Was Rebecca with you?"

"Aye. They grabbed her and drug her into those pine trees over there."

Isaac whipped out his phone, dialed 9-1-1 and handed his phone to the young man. "Tell them exactly what happened."

"Where are you going?"

Isaac heard a woman's scream in the distance. *Please, keep her safe until I get there.* "I'm going to help Rebecca. Now, get us some assistance!"

As Isaac ran toward the location of the scream, he saw the telltale trail. A sleeve, torn from a coat similar to Rebecca's, followed by the rest of the shredded wrap. An apron, also ripped. A white cap, just like his friend wore, crumpled. An abandoned athletic shoe. Black fabric, similar to the dress she always wore.

A woman's voice loudly begged from just ahead. "Please, please stop it. I don't want you to do this."

A man's laughter. "Quit fighting and it won't hurt as much."

The woman's voice was angry. "I said no! Get your hands off of me." The sound of a hand slapping against flesh split the silence of the trees.

"Why, you little..." An even louder sound of something hard against skin was accompanied by a woman's cry.

Isaac entered the trees in time to see Rebecca fly to the ground. Tommy Fuhrman grasped the girl by her long hair and yanked repeatedly.

The brute never saw it coming. Isaac grasped the thug's arm at the wrist and the elbow and violently slammed his knee in between.

The big man screamed from the pain of his broken bone. Isaac then grabbed the man's hair and smashed his forehead into the other man's mouth. Several quick punches to the chest sent the larger man flying into a bed of pine needles.

Isaac glanced at the girl. Her hair was down and Rebecca was trying to pull up the torn dress to cover herself.

"Are you okay?"

Her eyes widened and she screamed, "Look out! Behind you!"

From the corner of his eye, he caught a glimpse of the knife moving for his throat. Isaac threw his left arm up to cover his neck and it was lucky he did. The blade sliced deeply into his forearm, but the quick action saved his life.

Isaac rolled to his left, pivoted and drilled his fist into Matt Fuhrman's ribs. Fuhrman jabbed the knife into Isaac's shoulder. Isaac retaliated by crashing the heel of his hand against the big man's chin. Matt stumbled backwards.

Crouching, Isaac pinwheeled his leg around, taking the big man's feet out from under him.

"You son of a—" The first Fuhrman brother was on his feet and stumbled toward Isaac, but Isaac threw himself backwards into Tommy's chest. The big man was no match for the ex-Marine and was unconscious in seconds, even before he hit the ground.

Isaac walked over to where Matt was trying to get up. A quick kick to the head sent the man to la-la land.

"You're, you're bleeding." Rebecca was unstable as she stood. She held her ripped dress against her chest. Her long hair hung almost to her waist.

Seeing the blood running down his arm, he applied direct pressure and raised it in the air. "Head out to the road. I called 9-1-1 and handed the phone to your boyfriend."

"He's not my boyfriend. I need to stay and help you."

"No, get out to safety. When the police come, send them back here."

Rebecca glanced at the two villains. "What about those two men?"

"Them? They don't stand a chance. I'll keep them company. Now, please do as I asked and wait for the police."

"But, suppose they wake up?"

"Oh Rebecca, I don't understand you. They had no right to treat you like they did. Yet you're worried about them waking up? This may be a sin, but I pray to God they do."

***

Aubrey's heart was in her throat as she walked into the emergency room. The clerk led her back to the treatment room. A nurse was dressing her brother's left arm. A bandage was already taped on the left side of his chest. He smiled when he caught a glimpse of her. "Hey, Aubrey. How was your day?"

"A lot better now that I know you're okay. The police told me you'd been stabbed, and, and your arm was all cut up. The real question is how are you?"

"Phew. Don't worry about me. The stab wound missed anything important and I've had paper cuts worse than this one on my arm."

She had to wipe her cheek. "Do you think I'm dumb? I know you sugarcoat things so I don't worry. Why?"

"'Cause you're my little sister and I don't want to make you feel uncomfortable."

The nurse finished wrapping up his arm and reviewed the discharge instructions. Aubrey was still a little shaky as they walked to her mini-van. Isaac held the door, then climbed in next to her. "Does it hurt much?"

"No. The worst part was the stitches. I refused the meds to numb it."

"I'm glad it wasn't worse. How's Rebecca?"

"I don't know. She was gone by the time the police walked me out of the woods. That poor girl."

Aubrey reached across and touched his hand. "I'm glad you were there for her."

"I don't understand why people have to act that way. She never did anything to those two."

"Bullies stink. And the world's full of them."

He was silent for a few seconds. "That guy she was with? Do you know he was more interested in his horse than the fact they carried her off into the woods?"

"Not everyone has the same sense of honor that men like you and Connor do."

"Please tell me all Amish men don't act like that."

"Do all 'English' act like the Fuhrman brothers?"

He nodded. "Gotcha. Can I ask a favor?"

"Let me guess. Don't tell Leslie. Am I right?"

She almost laughed at his puzzled look. "How do you girls do this?"

"Do what?"

"Read my mind."

Now she did laugh. "That's something you'll need to research. So why don't you want me to tell my sister-in-law?"

"She dislikes Rebecca."

"I would, too, if I were in Leslie's shoes."

"Ouch!" He had banged his arm as he turned to face Aubrey. "Why would you dislike that girl?"

"Isaac, the girl wants you. Leslie views her as competition. That's why." She glanced at him. "You do need to tell Leslie about what happened. Besides, it's going to be hard hiding all those bandages."

"I could just wear long-sleeved shirts."

"Really? I over-estimated you, brother. With an attitude like that, you do *not* deserve to be with Leslie."

Isaac wiped his hand across his face. "I was trying to make a little joke. I will tell her, but I know because she's been hurt before, I'll need to do it in a way that won't make her upset. You know, so she doesn't feel that I jumped in to defend Rebecca—"

"But you did."

"Can I finish? That I didn't jump in to save Rebecca because I care for her. Like a lot. Like enough to make Leslie worry."

Aubrey lifted the turn signal and turned into her drive. "Okay. Mum's the word, but it might be hard keeping Grey from saying something to her." His bottom lip stuck out. "She's only nine."

A flash of brown in the mirror drew her attention. "Looks like we have visitors."

"Who?" She nodded at the closed buggy that had followed her in.

"I believe it's Rebecca... and her grandmother."

***

Isaac stepped from the mini-van and walked toward the buggy. Aubrey called to him, "I'll meet you inside."

"Thanks, sis."

The scent of a fireplace drifted down on him. Rebecca Stoltzfus climbed down from the buggy and walked until she stood in front of him. Her right eye was black and her cheek a dark purple. A tiny blot of dried blood was under her right nostril. She nodded. "Isaac."

"Rebecca. Does it hurt much?"

"My head's pretty sore and everything my right eye sees is foggy. My father said it will go away in time. And you? You bled real bad." She sniffed hard. "Truth is, I was so afraid you would die back there in that woods. How bad does your arm hurt?"

"It might throb a little, but it will pass. How is your friend? I know he was upset when the police put his horse down."

"Aaron just bought the poor thing this week. It was a Tennessee walking horse. Paid good money for it, too. And now it's gone."

"He seemed more concerned about the horse than you. I don't understand why he didn't try to protect you."

She shook her head and closed her eyes. "We live in different worlds, my English friend. We are peaceful. You are not, and today you showed the world that you are a true man, by English standards."

"I couldn't stand by and—"

She held her finger up. "I know, Isaac. And maybe I understand you a little better after today."

Her face contorted and her eyes welled. "I know what they were going to do to me. They kept telling me. Thank you for saving me." Rebecca wrapped her arms around him and squeezed tightly.

"I'm glad I was there for you."

The sound of an approaching vehicle caught his attention, until Rebecca grabbed his cheeks. "I love you, Isaac Golden, and I will until the day I die." He was unprepared for her lips against his. He gently pulled away and stared at her.

The voice of an old woman rolled out of the buggy. "Rebecca, you did what you wanted. Now, get back in the buggy. It's time to go home before Jacob and Amos come looking for us."

Rebecca's eyes were shiny. "Yes, grandmother." Quieter so only Isaac could hear, she questioned him. "Why couldn't you be plain or have at least accepted me as English, so we could be together? I'll never forget you or what you did today. Goodbye, Isaac Golden."

Rebecca climbed in the buggy and rode off. Isaac watched it fade into the darkening gloom of the night.

***

The irritating odor of the dairy farm filled the interior of the Suburban. Leslie giggled. *I've never been happier.* Spending the day shopping with her mom at the King of Prussia mall had been fun. Much to Leslie's surprise, her mom had treated her to lunch at a nice Mexican restaurant. But the best part of the day was about to happen—passing the evening time with Devo. *Doesn't matter what we do, I love spending time with him.* She'd realized she'd finally discovered her soulmate.

As Leslie turned onto the road where she lived, she saw the remnants of a flare as well as scars on the ground at the side of the road. Someone had skidded into the ditch. Leslie shook her head. People drove way too fast on this winding road. She just hoped no one got hurt.

Dusk was coming quickly. After all, today was the winter solstice. Starting tomorrow, the days would slowly grow longer. Her mind transported her to her favorite time of year—June. *Can't wait to dance in the moonlight with you, Devo.* Dreams she'd stored on a shelf for most of her life were finally coming true.

Connor and Aubrey's house appeared in the distance, standing like a lighthouse against the approaching dusk. The icicle lights Connor and Grey had strung on the barnyard fence flickered to life. She slowed, looking for Devo's truck. It was there all right, but her entire body chilled when she saw the other vehicle. Leslie braked to see what was happening. The sight turned her stomach. Devo and that Stoltzfus girl were embracing. And as she watched, they kissed.

Bitter anger flooded into every cell. *How could he?* Devo had told her there was nothing going on between him and that, that girl. But Leslie had seen it for herself. Devo's proclamation that his heart belonged to Leslie had been a lie. It was a good thing she was almost home because it was getting hard to see.

We're through. The long ramp to the front door had now become her personal Via Dolorosa, the path to her private prison—her solitary confinement.

Life had been so promising ten minutes ago and eternal happiness was simply a fruit, sweet and ripe for the picking. But it had withered and rotted on the vine right before her eyes. *Damn you, Devo.* All that crap about being devoted. Who was worse? Joe, the control freak or Devo, the liar? One was as bad as the other, but the cheating prevaricator was the one who'd torn her heart from her chest. *I hate you.*

In frustration, Leslie inserted the key and flung open the door. Immediately, the alarm system began squawking. She silenced it by depressing the button on her key fob. Thoughts of her brother and his family filled her mind. Aubrey was one of the closest friends she'd ever known. More of a sister to her than Grey's birth mother—Leslie's biological sister. Right now, Leslie wanted nothing more than to go over, give the man a piece of her mind and tell him to take that disgusting truck and his empty Marine Corps values and shove them... well, someplace she'd no longer have to see them. But she couldn't do that because the man she hated was Aubrey's brother. *God, this is going to be hard. Help me.*

The phone in her pocket started vibrating. Ripping it from her pants, she stared at it. On the display was a photo of them in front of her tree, taken just last week. After asking for strength again, she answered. "Hello?"

"Leslie, are you home yet?"

"Yeah, I just got here." *After witnessing the betrayal of the century.*

"How are you feeling? Did you have a good day with your mom?"

"I'm fine." *Except for that gaping hole in my back where you stabbed me.*

"How about I go pick up dinner before I stop by? If you find a good show on TV, I'll run and get the grub. Are you hungry for Chinese?"

How can he have this conversation like nothing happened? "And how was your day?"

He sighed. "It was a very rough day. I've got a lot to tell you."

Rough day, wasn't that what he said? *What, did Becky forget to use chapstick?* "Th-there's something I need to tell you, too."

"Want to wait until you can do it in person?"

"No."

"What? Why?"

"I had the opportunity today to analyze the last couple of weeks... and how this whole thing between us came about."

She could sense as well as hear the change in his voice. "Thing between us? What are you talking about?"

"You know, I got carried away and we went further than I ever should have allowed. I never should have let you kiss me. It dawned on me today why I did. It was only because I broke up with Joe, who I really, really loved." *Did that hurt? I hope so.*

"I, I, I don't understand."

Your chest ache yet? Mine sure does. "I was on the rebound. That's why you and I ended up together."

"Wait. I thought we had something special."

"Puh-lease. Did you really think I'd fall for some redneck mechanic, especially after dating a doctor? Did you? Honestly? If so, you're even denser than I thought."

"Okay. What happened?"

She kicked her shoes off and into the corner of the room. "I don't know what you mean."

"Tell me this is a joke."

"Do you hear me laughing?"

A long silence. *Say something so I can be mad at you.* "So, I take it you don't want to see me anymore?"

And here I thought you were a dumb *redneck.* "That's right. In fact, I don't so much as want to ever see you again. When there are family events, one of us should plan on being absent. And since I've got seniority in the family, I'm calling Christmas this year. Do you understand me?"

"Yes, ma'am. I'll make sure to stay out of your way."

"Fine."

"I read you, loud and clear. I have no idea what I did to anger you, but I'm sorry. If you want me gone, fine. I'm history. But I'm having trouble believing that's true. Is this what you really want?"

What I really want is a faithful man who doesn't want to control my life. "Yeah. Get out of my life. Forever."

***

Kim couldn't believe the buttons hadn't popped off his shirt. He was so proud of Rachel. All three shows had been perfect, going off without a problem. Every note, every word, each stage direction could be summed up in one word. *Perfect.* It was Sunday evening and the last performance had just ended. Kim was standing in line to wait his turn to shake the director's hand. *How long will I have to wait today?* Two hours on Friday night, almost three yesterday. Would he be willing to wait four hours tonight? *Yep, she's worth it.*

Rachel loved yellow roses. The bouquet he held in his arms contained three dozen of the aromatic flowers. Kim smiled. She'd received so many flowers last night that they wouldn't all fit in her Honda.

As he waited, Kim's mind drifted back to another woman... the first girl he'd ever loved. *Jenna.* She wasn't wild about flowers, unless they were lilies. Jenna had loved the scent so much that she'd searched and searched until she found a perfume which mimicked the sweet fragrance. He had yet to pass a lily without thinking about Jenna.

It struck him. *Wow.* This was probably the first time he'd thought about Jenna in a long time, maybe a month. And why? *Because I'm head over heels in love with Rachel.*

People were in a hurry to leave tonight. There was no school until after the New Year and everyone seemed quick to start their vacation. In only an hour and a half, the line had dwindled down to the last couple of stragglers. Finally, there were only three people ahead of him. He could see her features clearly now. Rachel was beaming, but Kim could readily see the exhaustion in her eyes. Two teenaged girls who'd had minor roles in the chorus finally said farewell and walked away. Just one more fan remained before she was all his.

But a chill rolled down his spine when he caught the look on Rachel's face and watched it turn pale. Her mouth was hanging open as she stared at the face of the man in front of him.

Kim stepped forward to see if he could recognize the guy, but no, he'd never seen him before. Kim turned when Rachel sobbed sharply. Her cheeks were wet. *What is going on?*

The man stood like a statue before Rachel. Kim could stand it no more.

"Excuse me, sir. Who are you?"

The man simply smiled. At Rachel.

Kim turned to her. "Do you know who this is?"

"Y-yes."

He waited, but she didn't continue. "Who is he, Rachel?"

"This is my love. My true love."

Being crushed by a runaway train wouldn't have hurt near as badly as hearing the woman he loved say those words. *About someone else.* Kim was sure he was staring at the man who'd once been Rachel's fiancé and almost her husband.

Kim's fists curled as he confronted the stranger. "Are you Eli?"

A smile now covered the man's face. The guy nodded slowly. "Yes. I am. No one's called me that in a long while, but it's true. I am Eli."

Please no. We've come so far. "And why are you here?"

"To correct the biggest mistake I ever made... leaving Rachel behind."

Rachel's hands now touched the man's face, her words a whisper. "It's you. It's really you. After all these years. I knew you'd come back."

"I couldn't stand it any longer. I needed to see you. We've wasted all these years, but I don't want to miss another second without you by my side. Come with me. I love you, Rachel."

Rachel wrapped her arms around the man who was a stranger to Kim. "I love you too, Eli."

I've lost her. Kim slowly walked away, dropping the huge bunch of flowers into the large can with the rest of the unwanted trash. Kim stumbled to the exit, but stopped to look at one of the play posters hanging by the door. It had caught his attention. Kim then quietly opened the door and walked into the cold night air. Snow was beginning to fall. He shook his head and muttered, "Yeah, ain't it a wonderful life?"

Chapter Fifteen

A ubrey was so excited. Tomorrow would be Cooper's first Christmas, not that he understood anything about the holiday, but still. Joy filled her heart. *Thank You, God, for all my blessings.* A shuffling noise behind her made her turn. *Isaac.* Her brother looked horrible this morning. "Merry Christmas and good morning."

He nodded. "Same to you, sis."

"It's awfully early. Why don't you go back to sleep?"

The man popped a pod in the Keurig. "I'm up now. Want a cup?"

"Yes, please. Don't you have off today?"

"That I do."

She walked over and rubbed his good arm. "Seriously, take the opportunity to sleep in."

"I don't seem to be able to sleep much these days. Besides, I wanted to have a private conversation with you."

Aubrey was pretty sure she knew what he wanted to talk about—Leslie. "You two really should talk this out."

He engaged her eyes and the thing she could see most was pain. "Our talking days are past."

"I think that—"

Isaac held up his hand. "Please don't. It hurts bad enough as it is. We're done."

"I don't believe that for one second. You two belong together. Made for each other, can't you see that? Connor and I do. Would you like me to help? Tonight, at the party—"

Again, he interrupted, but this time by putting his finger to her lips. "I'm glad I had the opportunity to reconnect with you. Sorry I missed out on this earlier in life. And I appreciate all you've done for me, but leave it be. I won't be here for the party tonight."

Her entire body quaked. "It's Christmas Eve. We'll all be here."

Isaac handed her the cup of black coffee. "Leslie made it clear. She doesn't want to be in the same room as me and, how'd she put it? Something like, 'When there's family events and holidays, one of us will have to stay away'. Then she told me Christmas was hers."

"No, this is unacceptable. What in blazes did you two fight about?"

He sipped his brew. "That's the thing—nothing. She told me she reconsidered... us... and realized she only turned to me because she was on the rebound from losing Joe. Then she reminded me how much she'd *loved* Joe and didn't say a word about me."

"No, no. Something's not right. I can tell you that's not true."

The pain in his eyes made Aubrey's own heart hurt. "It doesn't really matter anymore. Look, family means everything to me, sis. I know it does to you, too. And as long as I stick around, I'll be keeping you from enjoying your whole family."

"What are you trying to say? You do know you are part of my family, don't you?"

"If I'm at a family event, Leslie won't be. I've got no choice. Wouldn't be fair to you or Grey or Cooper."

"Isaac, I'm not following your line of reasoning."

He drained the rest of his cup in one long swig, then wiped his mouth with his sleeve. "I want you to know how grateful I am that you let me live here, but I've worn out my welcome. This was a special time in my life. One I'll remember forever." He rinsed the cup and placed it in the dishwasher. His eyes were focused aimlessly outside the window over the kitchen sink. "I've always wanted to see the Lone Star state. Decided to move to Texas. I need to give my notice with the Campbells, but then I'll get out of your hair. Your life can get back to normal."

"What? No. Stop this, right now. You are my family. It means so much to me, to all of us... you being here. Grey thinks the world of you. Don't you want to see her grow up into a lady? And who's going to teach Cooper how to work on cars? I haven't asked much of you the entire time you've been here, but I am now. *Stay.*"

He stared at her for a long period of time before shaking his head and then looking away. "I can't. You have no idea how much I'd like that, but no. It ain't happening."

"Isaac..."

"I, uh, I'll put the presents under the tree. Please make sure Grey gives Leslie the gift I got her, and take a mental picture of her reaction. Share it with me, someday."

"No. I want you to give it to her. Tonight."

"I can't. I won't be here."

"And exactly where will you be?"

"Company Christmas party. At the Tea Room."

"No, let's—"

His sudden movement caught her off guard. Isaac pulled her into a firm embrace. "Thank you for letting me live here with you for a little while. I thank God for giving me such a wonderful sister and I'm happy we had the chance to draw close, but... it's time for me to move on." He brushed his lips against her forehead. "Love ya, sis." And with that, he disappeared out the door.

***

Kim brushed the slush off of the polished stone. "I really made a fool of myself, Jenna." It was cold and according to the weatherman, was about to get colder. "They're predicting a white Christmas. I bet the celebration up there in Heaven is something to behold." Jenna always loved Christmas. "I hope you realize how much you spoiled me. People who are as honest as you, are rare." If he closed his eyes as tight as he could, Jenna's face would fill his imagination. But the problem was, as soon as he let up, just a little, Rachel's smile replaced Jenna's.

He gave up and opened his eyes. He traced the letters of her name. "Did I tell you Rachel's fiancé came back?" *God, this hurt, just like losing you.* "I can understand it, I guess. Imagine if one day I turned around and you were here. I'd hold you every second for the rest of my life. That's probably exactly how Rachel felt when she looked up and voila, there he was."

Kim knew it was his imagination, but he could swear the sweet scent of lilies was in the air. "How could I have been so stupid to ever think anyone but you would ever love me?" Snow flurries tickled his nose and he brushed them off his cheek.

"Your brother told me how you came back when he needed you most. He said you were his miracle. I don't understand the whole thing, but I could really use a miracle tonight, please? I don't think I've ever been this low. They say if you believe with all your heart, sometimes your wishes come true." *I'm crazy, pleading with a tombstone.* "I desperately need that miracle tonight, so I'll leave my door open for you. I love you, Jenna."

***

Leslie sat alone in front of the tree. An aura of despair seemed to have settled around her. Aubrey walked over and squeezed her sister-in-law's shoulder. "Where's Rachel?"

"I guess she's with Kim. I got a text from her Sunday evening that she was spending the night with her true love. Haven't seen her since. Some girls have all the luck, huh?"

"I guess. Want some hot chocolate?"

"Sure. Can I get some cookies to go with that?"

"Why not? It's Christmas."

Grey looked at her momma. "Can I have some, too?"

"If you can ask it both correctly and politely."

Grey crossed her arms. "Aunt Leslie didn't. Why do I?"

Aubrey shook her head. *Grey's so adorable.* "That's because Aunt Leslie doesn't have to put on a last-minute effort to impress Santa, like some little girl I know. Your aunt's been a good girl all year."

Leslie looked away and muttered, "Not so much."

Grey grabbed Aubrey's arm. "Momma, may I please go and get all of us some cookies and hot chocolate?"

The over-compensation was so obvious. "How 'bout we do it together? I'll get the drink and you find the sweets. We'll be back in a few minutes, sis."

When the pair returned, Aubrey noticed the picture Leslie had pulled up on her phone... and how slyly she wiped her cheeks. *I knew it!* Aubrey hadn't believed the story her brother told her this morning. If Leslie really didn't want to see Aubrey's brother anymore, why was she weeping over a picture of the two of them?

Within a few minutes, Grey's plate was empty. "Momma, can I have some more cookies, I mean *may* I have more cookies, please?"

"Not right now." She turned to Leslie. "I thought we'd eat when Connor gets back, okay?"

Leslie's gaze seemed focused on the tree. "Sure."

Aubrey felt the little girl's hand on her arm. "Can we open a present, Momma? Please?"

Great idea. "I think that's a wonderful thought." Aubrey walked to the tree and reached for a package that was the size of a hardback dictionary. "Grey, would you please give Aunt Leslie this gift?"

"I want one, too."

"Right after you give this to your aunt."

"Okay." Grey carried the package and handed it to Leslie. "Here you go."

Leslie took a deep breath and then shook her hands as if to dry them. "Okay. Thanks."

Aubrey knew what was inside. She'd wrapped it for her brother. "Wonder what it is?"

Leslie examined it. "I don't see a tag. Who could it be from?"

"Maybe if you open it, you'll know."

Grey piped up. "Come on, Aunt Leslie. Open the nativity set."

Aubrey touched her daughter's arm. "Don't spoil the surprise."

Leslie eyed them both strangely. "Is this something special?"

"Why don't you try removing the paper? That would be a novel idea."

Leslie shot Aubrey the stink eye. "Fine. Here goes." Leslie slipped her fingernail between the seams of the paper. She lifted the decorative covering away. Her face turned pale. "Oh my gosh." A sob escaped from her lips. "Look, it's never been opened." She displayed the exact 1951 Nativity set Grey had accidentally dropped. "Where did you find it?"

Aubrey shook her head. "I didn't get it."

"If you didn't, who did?"

"Isaac."

Leslie's chin quivered. She quickly stood and then ran into the kitchen.

Aubrey handed Grey a package. "Open this, honey."

Grey ripped the paper away and revealed a box of those plastic snap together building blocks. This one, when assembled, would build a princess castle. "Can I make this now?"

Aubrey kissed her daughter. "Sure, sweetie. I'm just going to see how Aunt Leslie's doing."

"Okay, Momma."

Aubrey hurried into the kitchen. Leslie was hunched over the sink, blotting moisture from her eyes. "Are you okay?"

"He found the exact set that was broken and bought one that was never opened. Why'd your brother have to be so thoughtful?" She twisted until she faced Aubrey. "Yet unfaithful."

"He told me this morning that you said you didn't want to see him anymore because you never really cared for him. That wasn't the truth, was it?"

Leslie shook her head.

"Why'd you lie to him?"

"I was paying him back. Like an eye for an eye."

"This doesn't make sense and... that's not like you."

"Devo told me I was the one he cared for." Leslie was having a hard time keeping her voice from quivering. "And what did I see?"

A light came on in Aubrey's mind. *I know.* "What do you think you saw?"

"I was driving back from Philly and when I came past your house, he and that, that girl were... He kissed her." She grabbed Aubrey's arms. "Ten minutes later, he calls and acts like nothing happened."

"Are you sure about this? I believe you've got it all wrong."

Leslie's lips turned into a fine white line, just before she spoke. "Why are you sticking up for him? I bet you didn't see them smooching."

"No, I'm not sticking up for him. I saw it, too. But do you know why *she*... kissed him?"

Leslie's eyes opened wide. "Wait. She kissed him... and you saw it?"

"Of course."

"Didn't that upset you or don't you care about me anymore?"

Aubrey shook her head. "What do you always say? 'Everything happens for a reason'. Do you know the reason?"

"There was a reason?"

"Of course! Did he explain what happened?"

"I didn't want him to know I saw them."

"Ah-ha. Then you don't know about the police or the thirty stitches he had to get to close the knife wounds?"

Leslie's face paled. "What? No. You're scaring me, Aubrey."

Aubrey shook her head. "You two are so alike, and you *both* need to work on better communication skills in the future."

"What happened?"

"You better sit down and listen. Isaac saved Rebecca's life. She stopped by to thank him. That's why she kissed him."

Chapter Sixteen

saac was seriously underdressed for the party. Both of his bosses were wearing tuxedos and many of the women looked like they'd just stepped off the red carpet. But despite what he was wearing, everyone made him feel welcome—from the lady with the accent who'd welcomed him to the older, heavyset woman who insisted he had to dance with her later. When Isaac returned to the table, his co-workers told him the lady was Henry Campbell's mother.

After loading a plate down with cheese, meatballs and shrimp, he sat next to two of his female co-workers. They tried to engage him in conversation, but he was too depressed. *I'll be leaving these friends behind, soon.* Not to mention his sister Aubrey, her family... and the girl he loved.

"Are you having a good time, Isaac?"

He spun to find Henry standing there. "Yes sir, thank you."

"We appreciate you coming to the cancer fundraiser tonight. Not sure if you knew it, but my sister-in-law had cancer and beat it. Not once, but twice."

"I hadn't heard."

"And see the big man over there?"

Isaac's mouth dropped open. "Is that who I think it is?"

Henry laughed. "Yes. Since you're a hockey fan I thought you might recognize him. The world knows him as a former NHL superstar, but we know him as Mickey Campeau. His daughter had a very rare form of cancer, but there she goes. Fit as a fiddle." Henry pointed to a little girl who streaked across the floor and jumped into her father's arms.

"Thank you for inviting me."

Henry winked at the girls sitting next to Isaac. "One of the ways we raise money is our dance auction, being held later. Isaac, would you mind being one of the bachelors whose dance card we auction off tonight? I understand my mum is going to start the bidding at twenty dollars for a dance with you."

"I, uh, well sure. It's for a good cause."

Henry shook his hand. "Thanks for being a good sport."

Just as Henry had indicated, a lady from the American Cancer Society gave a speech. Afterwards, a tiny woman with thick blonde hair spoke for a little while. Isaac hadn't met the man who stood behind her while she talked, but easily guessed it was Henry's brother because they looked so much alike. It was announced the man wrote children's books and the proceeds of any book sales for the night were going to the fundraiser. Isaac made sure to visit his table, and came away with two sets of books—one for Grey and one for Cooper.

Isaac had just settled down with some delicious looking whoopie pies when Henry took the microphone. "May I have everyone's attention? This evening, we have five eligible bachelors who have graciously agreed to have this evening's dance cards auctioned off." Henry stopped and turned to his wife. "As a reminder, you—Ellie Campbell—are not allowed to bid on any of them. Your dance card is permanently filled and belongs to me."

Everyone laughed. Ellie smiled and blew her husband a kiss. When Henry called the names of the victims, Isaac regretted agreeing to do this. *I don't know how to dance.* And even if he did, the woman he wanted to dance with wasn't here. One by one, the other four men went on the auction block. Their dance cards sold for around fifty dollars each.

Henry motioned for Isaac to stand next to him. In the distance the doorbell tinkled. "Ladies, we've saved the best for last. You see, he's my golden child, er, that is, his name is Isaac Golden. Rumor has it, his blood line can be traced back to Fred Astaire... or was it Benny Hill? Nevertheless, who will start the bidding for the opportunity to dance with Mr. Golden?"

As warned, Henry's mother waved a bill over her head. "I've got a twenty-spot for a Scottish jig."

To Isaac's surprise, one of the female co-workers who had sat next to him earlier countered with a bid ten dollars higher. She and Henry's mother alternated offers until the tender reached one hundred dollars. His co-worker blushed, shook her head and turned away.

Henry lifted the microphone again. "Ladies, one more chance. Do I hear more than one hundred dollars? Going once, going twice—"

A woman's voice from the back called out, "One thousand dollars. I bid one thousand dollars."

A collective gasp rose up from the crowd and everyone strained to see who called out the bid. Henry pointed in the direction of the mysterious woman. "Sold." He looked at his mother. "Sorry, mum. We'll take the money before the lady comes to her senses. You can dance with your other sons instead." Laughter and clapping ensued. Henry raised his hands. "Winning bidders, collect your prizes. This next dance is only for you. And the lady with the highest bid chooses the song. What song would you like, ma'am?"

Isaac's mouth dropped open when he saw the lady's identity. Her blue eyes were glowing and her voice was clear. "Please play 'All I Want for Christmas is You', by Vince Vance and the Valiants."

She approached and offered her hand. "Will you dance with me, Devo?"

He held her right hand and slipped his arm around her waist. "I, I thought you never wanted to see me again."

"I was mad. A little birdie said we need to work on our communication skills, so I was thinking, uh, how about we do that, say for rest of our lives. What do you think?"

Isaac was breathing heavy. "I would love that." Their lips blended together and nothing had ever felt better.

"Did you notice?"

"Notice what? The warmth of your lips?"

"No. It's snowing outside—a white Christmas and we have each other. It's like magic—Christmas magic. And on this night, maybe wishes really do come true."

***

Kim's eyes were glued to the broadcast. Despite having actually been there, he couldn't believe what the television station had done. The camera pans and closeups were spot on. Okay, the volume weakened one or two places, but for the most part, it was perfect. And the commentary provided by both Didi Phillips-Zinn and Rachel was tasteful... and touching.

Kim's vision turned wavy when the newscaster talked about what the show meant to her. How there was hope even in your moment of deepest despair. And the human capacity to love one another made it all worthwhile. Didi spoke about her husband, missing in battle almost two years and that the community of friends and family were the rock she clung to and how they helped get her through.

Then it was Rachel's turn. He recognized the décor. The interview had been filmed at the Essence of Tuscany Tea Room. Rachel seemed so happy and her beauty filled the screen. "This play holds a special place in my heart because it tells my story. All the special things I wanted to do, never happened. Just like with George Bailey, something else always came up to rob my happiness, or so I thought. You have to understand, I believe there's a purpose behind everything, no coincidences. I went through so many hardships before I came here."

Rachel paused to dab her eyes. "And when I came here, I found all the things I thought I'd lost—family, friendship and love. But just like our character George, I failed to see how blessed... and loved I am. I used to will things to be different... for so many personal events to have never happened." Rachel again wiped her cheeks. "But my eyes were opened when my guardian angel rescued me. He thawed my cold heart and gave me love where it wasn't expected. So, I dedicate this show to the man who is my real-life guardian angel. Thank you, my closest friend and Merry, Merry Christmas." Rachel's voice faded to a bell ringing.

Didi Phillips-Zinn then patted Rachel's hand and turned to the camera. "Thank you for tuning in tonight. And now, the conclusion of *It's a Wonderful Life*. From all of us here at the station, Merry Christmas and Happy Holidays."

Kim's eyes were too wet to focus on the rest of the play. All he could think about was Rachel. He dropped to his knees. "Father God, tonight, I ask but two things. One prayer is for my friend Rachel. Please grant her every happiness she has coming... love, life, health, old age and especially love. If I've earned any blessing in this life, bequeath it to her."

He wiped his arm across his face. "I'm ashamed to ask you this second thing, Lord. I can't take this anymore. First, losing my Jenna and now, Rachel's gone. I've never felt this low and I don't know what to do. Please, take this cup from me and grant me a miracle. I feel like I'm dying and I want to live, but I don't think I have the strength to go on. Help me, Lord."

He felt a breeze in the room, as if someone had opened the door. The strong scent of lilies filled the room. One of his windchimes echoed through the night. The warm touch against his face normally would have startled him. But Kim knew it was either the miracle he'd prayed for or else his new reality. And that reality was that he had finally crossed the line to insanity. And it didn't matter which it was. *Please, don't let it stop.* It was no surprise when warm arms enfolded him. *Can't open my eyes.* This was what he'd asked for, his miracle. *Please don't ever let this moment end.*

A quiet voice whispered in his ear. "I was wrong."

That's not Jenna's voice. His eyes flew open. The arms still held him. Warm lips touched his neck. Kim broke free, stood and whipped around. "Rachel?"

She nodded and kissed him. "Forgive me. I made a huge mistake."

"I thought you left with, with *him*."

She held his cheeks. "I did, and we made it as far as Des Moines. But there was a problem."

"Problem?"

"Yes. With every mile we drove west, the feeling grew until I admitted it to myself. And I knew I was wrong."

"About what?"

Her cheeks were wet. "Eli wasn't my true love. *You are.* Kim, take me back, please. I want to—"

He placed his finger against her lips. His heart was beating so rapidly, it threatened to burst through his chest. "Rachel, Rachel... Do you know what just happened here, tonight?"

"What are you talking about?"

"I prayed for a miracle and believed with all my heart. And, and it happened. God granted my prayer. *You* are my Christmas miracle."

Rachel kissed him again. "A miracle? No. This is where I belong, if you'll have me—"

He couldn't help but smile. "Like you said in the interview, everything happens for a reason. You and me, we were meant to be. I love you, Rachel. Please, stay with me forever."

She nodded her head. "That's the plan."

He hugged her tightly. His windchimes outside had never rung as loudly. "And now, I can truly say... It's a wonderful life."

Epilogue

Summary Solstice

Summer Solstice

Leslie carried the sliced zucchini and sweet corn on the tray. The boisterous tweeting of the songbirds was the soundtrack of happiness on this, the longest day of the year. She couldn't help but smile at the man turning the steaks on the grill.

He pivoted and shot her that smile, the one that made her feel giddy. "Hey, beautiful. Need some help?" Devo took the tray and placed it on the grill-side table. His strong arms pulled her against him. "I love you, my evening star."

"I love you, too." Their lips met, sending fireworks through her mind. But the sound of a car horn disrupted their embrace.

Connor stepped from the mini-van and called, "Get a room, you two."

Devo waved. "Hey, bro."

Leslie squeezed her husband's hand. "Figures. He's been a bother since the day he was born. Always has to interrupt all the fun things."

Devo gestured at Aubrey when she climbed out. He whispered only loud enough for Leslie to hear. "Thankfully he doesn't live in this house anymore. There are certain things that just can't be interrupted." He bounced his hip against her. "If you get my drift, pumpkin."

She grasped his face and kissed him. "Did I mention I love you?"

"Yuck. Momma! Uncle Devo and Aunt Leslie are kissing again." Grey stood in front of them, hands on her hips. "Is supper ready yet?"

Aubrey carried Cooper in her arms, but she directed the comment at her daughter. "Sweetheart, you'll have to forgive them. They're newlyweds."

Connor brought over a bowl of Amish macaroni salad. "Grey, do you know why Aunt Leslie married Uncle Devo on February fourteenth?"

Grey was wearing her new glasses and when she looked at her adopted daddy, the spectacles gave her the appearance of being cross-eyed. "Because it's Valentine's Day?"

"Nope. It's because it's the same day Momma and I married. That way she won't have to remember her anniversary on her own. That's a college-girl trick. When you grow up, maybe you can go to Millersville University, like I did."

Leslie nudged Devo and smiled at Connor. "You can go anywhere you want, sweetheart. But you've got to watch out for those university boys." She stuck her tongue out at her brother. "At least I didn't marry my sister, like you did."

Connor's eyes narrowed, but a smile tugged at his lips. "I married my wife before she became my sister."

Aubrey cleared her throat. "Sister-in-law, thank you."

A white car pulled up. Kim and Rachel Landis spilled out. Leslie bounced over and hugged her friend. "Look, everybody. It's the other newlyweds, back from their honeymoon. How was St. Johns?"

Rachel's face turned pink. "Fine. What little we saw of it."

Aubrey also hugged Rachel. "Welcome home. To celebrate your homecoming, I iced a bottle of wine."

Before long, Devo had the food ready and the group settled around the outdoor patio Leslie and Devo had built. He cleared his throat and removed his ever-present Vikings cap. Devo then reached for the hands of the two closest people—his wife Leslie and his sister Aubrey. "Let's take a moment and give thanks." He bowed his head. "Dear Father in Heaven, we want to thank You for all the blessings here tonight. And while we're thankful for the bounty of the food on this table, the thing we're most thankful for is the love of friends who've become a family, and family that are friends. And I'm sure You are laughing up there in Heaven, because this place that's called Paradise truly is paradise. I believe You've given us a glimpse of Heaven and how You want us to live. Thank You for so many, many blessings. Amen."

Everyone echoed Devo's last word, except Cooper. He simply chattered, "Da-da, Da-Da, Da-da."

When all of their appetites were satisfied, Connor grabbed a large bag from the van. "Who wants to have a water gun battle?"

Leslie shook her head and smiled when Grey grabbed the biggest squirter and sprayed the men. Grey took off around the corner of the house, screaming with glee. The three men laughed as they gave chase.

Aubrey sighed as she watched the ruckus. "My brother's prayer was beautiful and so true. I never thought I could be this happy." She glanced at the other two women. "And I'm glad we get to share this together."

Leslie giggled. "I remember the day I brought you here."

Rachel laughed. "I do, too. Aubrey thought that Connor had planned it all out and had evil intentions."

"Yes, but as I look back now, I realize it was God who had it planned out, not Connor. The same plan He had to bring you and Kim together. And help Leslie and Isaac fall in love. My older brother was right. This is a glimpse of Heaven, our Paradise."

After everyone said goodnight, Leslie and Devo sat in their zero-gravity chairs, watching the stars. Devo kissed her hand and then stood. "I think it's time to cross something off your bucket list. I'll be right back."

My bucket list? He returned shortly, carrying an ancient boom box. "Where'd you dig up that monstrosity?"

"I bought it at an antique shop." He held up a cassette. "Got it so I could play this thing." He extended his hand. "Love of my life, would you do me the everlasting pleasure of dancing with me under the stars? I'll have you know, my dance card only belongs to you."

"Then I got a bargain, didn't I?" Leslie's mind drifted back to last Christmas Eve and the magic of the evening. The night of the three big surprises. At the end of "All I Want for Christmas is You," Isaac dropped to his knees and held her hands. The entire tea room grew silent as she gazed into his eyes. The first surprise was upon her.

"Leslie, there's no logical reason I can think of for you to say yes. I don't have a ring. I didn't get a chance to ask your mom's permission. We're so different. You're smart, beautiful, funny and I'm a dumb hillbilly. I have nothing to offer you but my heart. But I need to ask... I want to grow old with you. Will you marry me?"

The second surprise occurred exactly eleven point three nanoseconds after his words reached her eardrum. Before her brain had a chance to process the proposal, her heart answered for her. *"Yes, yes."* She had dropped to her knees to kiss the man she loved, her soulmate.

They had immediately left the Tea Room and driven to the party Aubrey was hosting. She'd never forget her family's reaction or the third surprise of the evening. The one when Rachel and Kim came barreling in and the words that flowed from Rachel's lips. *"We've got an announcement to make. We're engaged."*

Devo pulled her close, returning her to the present. Leslie didn't recognize the song until she heard the sweet voice of Michelle Phillips. "This, this song, it's one of my favorites. I used to play this on my phone every night, dreaming someday I'd look up and the man of my dreams would be there." She gently kissed her husband. "And it finally came true."

He rubbed his nose against hers. "I know. I had a hard time finding that cassette."

She searched his eyes. "How did you know about this?"

"Your brother mentioned it to me. Once you get past all the teasing the two of you do, Connor loves and wants only the best for you. He's a good man and I'm so happy he and Aubrey found each other."

"I don't want to talk about him. Not during this song."

His smile melted her heart once again. "And why's that?"

"Because just like it says, this song is 'dedicated to the one I love'—you. I love you."

Devo's lips again touched hers. "I love you."

"You were right, you know?"

That deep laugh raised her pulse. "About what?"

Before she could answer, a shooting star lit the night. Leslie's heart was completely full. *God's exclamation point.* "This place and time. It truly is paradise."

The End

Get exclusive

never-before-published content!

www.chaswilliamson.com

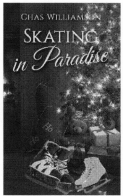

A Paradise Short Story

Download your free copy of
Skating in Paradise today!

Other Books by this Author

Seeking Forever (Book 1)
Kaitlin Jenkins long ago gave up the notion of ever finding true love, let alone a soulmate. Jeremy is trying to get his life back on track after a bitter divorce and an earlier than planned departure from the military. They have nothing in common, except their distrust of the opposite sex.

An unexpected turn of events sends these two strangers together on a cross-country journey—a trip fraught with loneliness and unexpected danger. And on this strange voyage, they're forced to rely on each other—if they want to survive. But after the past, is it even possible to trust anyone again?

Seeking Forever is the first book of Chas Williamson's Seeking series, the saga of the Jenkins family over three generations.

Will Kaitlin and Jeremy ever be the same after this treacherous journey?

Seeking Happiness (Book 2)

Kelly was floored when her husband of ten years announced he was leaving her for another woman. But she isn't ready to be an old maid. And she soon discovers there's no shortage of men waiting in line.

Every man has his flaws, but sometimes the most glaring ones are well hidden. And now and then, those faults can force other people to the very edge, to become everything they're not. And when that happens to her, there's only one thing that can save Kelly.

Seeking Happiness is the second book of Chas Williamson's Seeking series, the saga of the Jenkins family over three generations.

Ride along with Kelly on one of the wildest adventures you can imagine.

Seeking Eternity (Book 3)

At eighteen, Nora Thomas fell in love with her soulmate and best friend, Stan Jenkins. But Nora was already engaged to a wonderful man, so reluctantly, Nora told Stan they could only be friends. Stan completely disappeared (well, almost), from her world, from her life, from everywhere but Nora's broken heart.

Ten painful years later, the widow and mother of two was waiting tables when she looked up and found

Stan sitting in her section. But she was wearing an engagement ring and Stan, a wedding ring. Can a woman survive when her heart is ripped out a second time?

Seeking Eternity is the third book of Chas Williamson's Seeking series, a glimpse at the beginning of the Jenkins' family saga through three generations.

Will Nora overcome all odds to find eternal happiness?

Seeking the Pearl (Book 4)

Eleanor Lucia has lived a sad and somber life, until she travels to London to open a hotel for her Aunt Kaitlin. For that's where Ellie meets Scotsman Henry Campbell and finally discovers true happiness. All that changes when Ellie disappears without a trace and everyone believes she is dead, well almost everyone.

But Henry and Ellie have a special bond, one that defies explanation. As if she were whispering in his ear, Henry can sense Eleanor begging him to save her. And Henry vows he will search for her, he will find her and he will rescue her, or spend his last breath trying.

Seeking the Pearl is the exciting finale of Chas Williamson's Seeking series, the culmination of the three generation Jenkins' family saga.

Henry frantically races against time to rescue Ellie, but will he be too late?

Whispers in Paradise (Book 1)

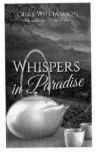

Ashley Campbell never expected to find love, not after what cancer had done to her body. Until Harry Campbell courts her in a fairy tale romance that exceeds even her wildest dreams. But all that changes in an instant when Harry's youngest brother steals a kiss, and Harry walks in on it.

Just when all her hopes and dreams are within reach, Ashley's world crumbles. Life is too painful to remain in Paradise because Harry's memory taunts her constantly. Yet for a woman who has beaten the odds, defeating cancer not once, but twice, can anything stand in the way of her dreams?

Whispers in Paradise is the first book in Chas Williamson's Paradise series, stories based loosely around the loves and lives of the patrons of Sophie Miller's Essence of Tuscany Tea Room.

Which brother will Ashley choose?

Echoes in Paradise (Book 2)

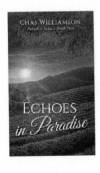

Hannah Rutledge rips her daughters from their Oklahoma home in the middle of the night to escape a predator from her youth. After months of secrecy and frequent moves to hide her trail, she settles in

Paradise and ends up working with Sam Espenshade, twelve years her junior. Sam wins her daughters' hearts, and earns her friendship, but because of her past, can she ever totally trust anyone again?

Yet, for the first time since the death of her husband, Hannah's life is starting to feel normal, and happy, very happy. But a violent attack leaves Sam physically scarred and drives a deep wedge between them. To help heal the wounds, Hannah is forced from her comfort zone and possibly exposes the trail she's tried so hard to cover.

Echoes in Paradise is the second book in Chas Williamson's Paradise series, an exciting love story with Sophie Miller's Essence of Tuscany Tea Room in background.

When the villain's brother shows up on Hannah's doorstep at midnight on Christmas night, were the efforts since she left Oklahoma in vain?

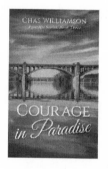

Courage in Paradise (Book 3)

Sportscaster Riley Espenshade returns to southcentral Pennsylvania so she can be close to her family while growing her career. One thing Riley didn't anticipate was falling for hockey's greatest superstar, Mickey Campeau, a rough and tall Canadian who always gets what he wants... and that happens to be Riley. Total bliss seems to be at her fingertips, until she discovers Mickey also loves another girl.

The "other girl" happens to be Molly, a two-year old orphan suffering from a very rare childhood cancer. Meanwhile, Riley's shining career is rising to its zenith when a new sports network interviews her to be the lead anchor. Just when her dream job falls into her lap, Mickey springs his plan on her—a quick marriage, adopting Molly and setting up house.

Courage in Paradise is Chas Williamson's third book in the Paradise series, chronicling the loves and lives of those who frequent Sophie Miller's Essence of Tuscany Tea Room.

Riley is forced to make a decision, but which one will she choose?

Stranded in Paradise (Book 4)

When Aubrey Stettinger is attacked on a train, a tall, handsome stranger comes to her assistance, but disappears just as quickly. Four months later, Aubrey finds herself recuperating in Paradise at the home of a friend of a friend.

When she realizes the host's brother is the hero from the train, she suspects their reunion is more than a coincidence. Slowly, and for the first time in her life, Aubrey begins to trust—in family, in God and in a man. But just when she's ready to let her guard down, life once again reminds her she can't trust anyone. Caught between two worlds, Aubrey must choose between chasing her fleeting dreams and carving out a new life in this strange place.

Stranded in Paradise is the fourth book in the Paradise series, chronicling the loves and lives of those who frequent Sophie Miller's Essence of Tuscany Tea Room.

Will Aubrey remain *Stranded in Paradise*?

Christmas in Paradise (Book 5)
True love never dies, except when it abandons you at the altar.

Rachel Domitar has found the man of her dreams. The church is filled with friends and family, her hair and dress are perfect, and the honeymoon beckons, but one knock at the door is about to change everything.

Leslie Lapp's life is idyllic – she owns her own business and home, and has many friends – but no one special to share her life... until one dark and stormy afternoon when she's forced off the highway. Will the knock at her door be life changing as well?

When love comes knocking at Christmas, will they have the courage to open the door to paradise?

About the Author

Chas Williamson's lifelong dream was to write. He started writing his first book at age eight, but quit after two paragraphs. Yet some dreams never fade...

It's said one should write what one knows best. That left two choices—the world of environmental health and safety... or romance. Chas and his bride have built a fairytale life of love. At her encouragement, he began writing romance. The characters you'll meet in his books are very real to him, and he hopes they'll become just as real to you.

True Love Lasts Forever!

Follow Chas on
www.bookbub.com/authors/chas-williamson

Enjoyed this book?
Please consider placing a review on Amazon!